I0654926

Published by Lift Bridge Publishing

Copyright © 2015 by Ramona Mejia

All Rights Reserved

Library of Congress Cataloging-in-Publication Data

Mejia, Ramona

Destiny

ISBN 978-0-9961536-9-0

PRINTED IN THE UNITED STATES OF AMERICA

FIRST EDITION

Acknowledgements

Thank you, first and foremost, to my Lord and Savior, Jesus Christ. He said in His Word (Proverbs 18:16) that my gift would make room for me—what an awesome promise for this newbie author! He has been so faithful, I pray that His will continues to be done in my life.

To those who prayed for me, cheered me on and recognized that I had a gift (even when I thought it was just a fun hobby)—with my whole heart, I thank you.

My beloved husband, John, who believed in me from the very first—thank you for believing in this dream of mine, even when we didn't know when or how it would ever come to pass: we've come a long way, baby!

My Mom, Gladys, who nurtured and inspired the dreamer in me and has always challenged me to be the best that I can be and to trust in God no matter what: thank you for being the wind beneath my wings!

My dear cousin, Donyale (seriously, I've bounced more storylines off of this young lady): Donie, I finally did it—I'm a published author!

My cousin, Derek, who only read one chapter and said that he could imagine this story being made into a movie—*thanks for the ego boost, little cuz!*

My SICs (Sisters in Christ): Pam, Keisha, Gwen, Franka, Gaileen, Janet, Ruth, Carolyn and Sharmayne: I've known you throughout various seasons of my life...thank you for your prayers, for laughter, for being sounding boards, for inspiring words and for being that kick in the pants which I sometimes needed to quit procrastinating!

To Stef: thanks for having the patience and good humor to sit and answer some of my "cop" questions (I still owe you a better cup of coffee)!

To graphic artist extraordinaire, Natasha Miller of K&T Graphics, I kid you not: this lady has the patience of Job! Thank you for your amazing ability to get inside my head and bring my vision to life—whether it's in the form of a book cover, or a trailer—you rock, girl!

A special thank you to Pastor Tara Owens, an amazing woman of God who dares to dream big and believe God for the greater. Thank you for just being you (and for being real). *We are destined for greatness!*

And last, but certainly not least, to my publisher, Ashley Graham of Lift Bridge Publishing, who read an excerpt from this novel and said, "We have to get you published right away!" Thank you for educating me and for believing in this gift that God has given to me and for doing what you do on a daily basis in excellence…may He bless the work of your hands in ways that you couldn't even begin to ask or imagine, in Jesus' name!

destiny [des-t*uh*-nee]

Noun.

1. Something that is to happen or has happened to a particular person or thing; lot or fortune.

2. The predetermined, usually inevitable or irresistible, course of events.

3. The power or agency that determines the course of events.

4. (*Initial capital letter*) this power personified or represented as a goddess.

"destiny." *Dictionary.com Unabridged*. Random House, Inc. 19 Nov. 2015. <Dictionary.com http://dictionary.reference.com/ browse/destiny>.

Chapter 1

"Get in!" the officer yelled, as he flung the door open on the passenger side and the woman dove in, toppling a couple of stunned journalists in the process. Fortunately, Saturday afternoon traffic on Park Avenue wasn't as busy as it was during the week. The streets were clear as the RMP burned rubber and the Four Seasons Hotel quickly disappeared from view.

The cop's impromptu guest breathed a shaky sigh of relief. "Thank you, officer, you've got great timing!"

"No problem, glad I was able to help. Hope you don't mind my asking, but what happened to your security detail?"

The woman shook her head, as she shakily fastened the seatbelt. "They must've gotten swallowed up by that mob."

"Someone tipped off the press," he said as a matter of fact.

"Yeah, so much for a quiet brunch in my favorite part of town!"

"Is there somewhere I can drop you off?" he asked, stealing a glance at her. Destiny Jordan was every bit as gorgeous in person as she was on the small screen. Flawless tawny skin, almond-shaped eyes a shade of chocolate you had to see to believe, full lips, streaked honey blond hair and a figure that only an airbrush could emulate.

In his line of work, seeing pretty women in the 'city that never sleeps' was commonplace, but this particular woman was something special. She was an *international* recording star and he had just rescued her from a crowd of frenzied fans and paparazzi.

"I don't want you to go out of your way, you've done so much already," she said graciously, surveying the damage to her person in a MAC compact. She'd lost one of her favorite chandelier earrings during that scary little episode and a pocket on her Nicole Miller fur was torn. Granted, things could have been worse. Much worse.

"It's no problem. I was heading back to the precinct when I saw that you were in trouble. I'm off for the rest of the evening."

"In that case, First Avenue and the Upper East Side,

officer—"

"Reilly. Mike Reilly."

"Please...call me Destiny," she said with a tremulous smile.

Security was tight in her building. In addition to two doormen, there were uniformed security guards seated behind a console which concealed some very sophisticated surveillance equipment. Obviously the recording star wasn't the only VIP living in the trendy condominium.

When Mike entered the building with Destiny the head guard immediately stood up and came over to find out what was going on. It wasn't every day that one of the residents walked in with a uniformed policeman. Destiny reassured the guard that everything was fine, gave him a brief synopsis of what had occurred and informed him that Mike would be escorting her upstairs. The guard suggested that she use one of his personnel, but Destiny insisted on Mike.

It was a quiet elevator ride, as Mike took note of the high-tech design in the plush car. You couldn't even get off on a floor that you didn't live on. He could only imagine what one of the condos must have cost. The security alone had to be a fortune.

Outside her front door, Mike paused. "You'll be fine from here, right?"

"Do you have to leave right away?" Destiny blurted. "I mean—my assistant will be here soon!" A faint blush stained her cheeks. She was practically stuttering! *What was the matter with her?*

"I suppose I can stay a little while longer," he replied, trying to put her at ease.

"Thanks, I'm usually not this jumpy. I guess today's incident shook me up more than I realized." She used an access card to open the front door of her condo, which happened to be on the twenty-fifth floor of the thirty-story building.

Following her into the spacious, softly-lit living area, Mike was pleased to discover that not all recording stars decorated

6

their homes like those featured on MTV's *Cribs* show. He was expecting a space filled with extravagance and framed hit records obliterating a couple of walls...not inviting yellow and blue toile and distressed antique-white furnishings.

Destiny noticed the appreciative gleam in his eyes. "It's French Country. I wish I could take credit for choosing each piece, but I had it done professionally."

"I like it. It sort of reminds me of my Aunt Sophia's place," he said with a little smile.

Destiny lost her train of thought. She was about to tell him that the guy who'd designed her place had been born in Provence, France...

Officer Reilly had dimples.

Collecting herself, she took off her fur and placed it carefully over the back of a mahogany chair with cabriole legs. "Would you like something to drink, Officer Reilly?"

"No, thank you."

"You are off duty, aren't you?" she asked, raising a perfectly sculpted eyebrow.

"Yes, but I still have to go back to the precinct, fill out some paperwork and return my vehicle."

"Right," she said pensively. "Well I'm going to get out of these heels and pour myself a glass of wine. Please, make yourself at home."

Mike called his sergeant and informed him about the unusual turn of events. He had already notified Central about the mob situation at the restaurant on Park; by now it had already been contained.

Destiny watched the policeman on a surveillance monitor in her bedroom. Her guardian angel was talking on his iPhone. A six-foot-two angel with dark chocolate hair and eyes the color of tropical water. She had no idea that a cop could look that way and still take the job seriously. She wondered if he tore open the shirt of his uniform if there'd be an 'S' emblazoned across his chest. Officer Reilly intrigued her.

Destiny's personal assistant, Chelsea, arrived as promised thirty minutes later. When she walked through the front door and saw the policeman she was speechless—a rare occurrence for the highly-opinionated assistant.

"Chelsea, this is Officer Mike Reilly," Destiny said suppressing a grin. "Officer Reilly, my personal assistant, Chelsea Bryant."

The assistant shook the cop's hand and tried not to stare. "Pleased to meet you," she mumbled.

"Same here, Ms. Bryant," he said politely and then turned to Destiny. "Now that the cavalry's arrived—"

"Do you have to leave?" she asked before she could catch herself.

Mike felt the corners of his lips twitching with amusement. "Yes. You ladies have a good evening."

"Thanks again, Officer Reilly…for everything," Destiny said resisting the urge to hug him.

Mike nodded slightly. "You're welcome."

Chelsea gave a low whistle after he left. "Man! Now that's what I call serving *and* protecting!"

"Can you believe him?" Destiny exclaimed, rushing over to the window to catch a glimpse of the cop getting into his car. "He should be working at Chippendales, not a precinct!"

"The question should be can I believe *you*!" Chelsea replied with a knowing look.

"What?" Destiny blinked innocently.

"You like him—don't try to deny it."

"Why would I deny it? You saw him! That *was* 'New York's Finest' and he's totally unaffected by me. He really was just doing his job!"

"And he didn't try to make a pass at you or say something stupid?" Chelsea asked skeptically.

"He was a perfect gentleman the entire time. He wouldn't even let me make him a drink!"

"Sooo, when are you going to see him again?"

"Hopefully next weekend and you're going to arrange it!"

Hardly anyone knew what Destiny's personal assistant looked like and that always worked in her favor. Chelsea was making a special trip to Mike's precinct in person. The media watched just about every move Destiny made whenever she left her building and sending a courier with the invitation was just too risky. What if it ended up in the hands of someone who wanted to sell the information? Chelsea wasn't taking any chances.

She just hoped that the cop was available and that he wouldn't laugh her out of the building. *What if he wasn't interested?*

Chelsea forced herself to relax; she was getting worked up for nothing. There wasn't a red-blooded male alive who could resist Destiny. Everything would be fine. The cop seemed like an average guy—above average in the looks department—but an average guy, nonetheless. He didn't seem like the type who would embarrass Chelsea or send her packing.

The driver pulled up beside the precinct and parked the Town Car.

"Back in fifteen, Sam," Chelsea promised, as she exited the shiny black vehicle with tinted glass.

The driver nodded knowingly and flipped open a copy of *The Times.*

When Chelsea entered the squat brick building a barrage of noise greeted her. Trying not to appear as anxious as she felt, she ignored the suspects being hauled away to interrogation rooms, or holding cells, and the blinding fluorescent lighting and walked directly over to a countered window where an officer was stationed. "Good afternoon, officer."

"Afternoon, Ma'am. How can I help you?" he asked.

"I need to speak with Officer Mike Reilly."

"Is he expecting you?"

"No."

"May I ask what this is regarding?" the officer asked, trying not to look bored. It had been a surprisingly quiet day on the switchboard and he was due to go on break soon. He hoped business with this civilian ended quickly.

"It's actually a personal matter," Chelsea replied.

"You don't have to go into details, Ma'am, but—"

Chelsea took a deep breath and forged ahead. "I'm going to assume that you've heard of Destiny, the recording star."

"She's practically a household name," the officer said with a lazy grin, obviously pleased with himself for being in the know.

"Well, I'm her personal assistant and I have a message for Officer Reilly from her."

"How do I know you're on the up and up?" the cop asked lightly.

"You're just going to have to take my word for it. I met Officer Reilly the day he rescued Destiny from that mob. Would you like to see my business card?"

"Okay, okay, hold on a minute," he said, signaling a young officer passing by. "Sanchez, do me a favor and tell Reilly to come to the front desk. Destiny Jordan's *personal assistant* wants to speak with him!"

Chelsea wanted to disappear. Everyone within hearing distance turned to get a glimpse of her. She half expected them to come over and ask for autographs. When the moment passed uneventfully, she thanked the cop behind the window and did her best to ignore the amused expression on his ruddy face.

Five minutes later Officer Reilly came down a flight of stairs and Chelsea couldn't help staring—the man could certainly wear a uniform. It was almost unfair that Destiny had stumbled across this one.

"Lady says she knows you, Reilly," the window cop said by way of explanation.

"Thanks, O'Connor. Chelsea, it's nice to see you again," Mike said with a polite smile. "Is everything alright?"

"Hello, Officer Reilly. Everything's fine, thank you. I'm sorry to show up at your precinct uninvited—"

"That's actually a good thing," he jokingly replied.

The other officer was knee deep in their conversation. Chelsea decided that she'd had enough of him for one day. "Is there somewhere we can speak privately?" she asked Mike.

"Sure, follow me."

10

They went into an empty office down the hall and Chelsea couldn't help but think that it looked just like the ones she'd seen in a couple of her favorite police shows.

Did they all use the same painter and decorator?

"I'm not getting you in trouble, am I?" Chelsea asked with a sudden look of concern.

"No, Chelsea. We are allowed to take breaks between chasing down the bad guys," he said with a warm smile. "So, what can I do for you?"

"I wanted to drop this off," she replied, handing him a small ivory-hued envelope. "I didn't want to leave it with just anyone."

"What is this?" he asked, accepting the sealed envelope and instantly recognizing the scent on it. Destiny had been wearing it day he met her.

"Destiny wants to thank you for everything you did for her the other day…over dinner. You don't have to confirm right this minute, of course. She knows that it's really short notice; all of the information is on the invite. If you would just call before the week is out to confirm it would be appreciated."

"This is really nice of her," Mike said sincerely. "Tell her that she doesn't have to do this."

"Believe me, Officer Reilly, it would be her pleasure."

When Mike went downstairs to the locker room to change back into his street clothes, five officers he'd gone to the academy with started singing a catchy R&B tune and pointing in his direction. Another one started doing some hip-hop steps and batting his eyelashes at him.

"What's going on around here? Has everybody gone crazy?" Mike asked no one in particular.

"Reilly's the man!" one rookie replied, as he high-fived another officer on his way out of the locker room.

"What are they talking about?" Mike asked his partner of five years, as he put his uniform away.

Officer Dave Ramirez held up a copy of *The Post*. The front page boasted a photo of Mike rescuing international recording star, Destiny, from a frenzied mob. "I leave you alone for one day and this is what you're up to?"

Groaning, Mike banged his head against the locker. "They're never gonna let me live this one down, are they?"

"No, this'll definitely take a minute. So tell me, is she really as gorgeous in person as she is in her videos?"

"More than gorgeous—but, you know something? She's nice, too."

"She didn't expect to be waited on hand and foot like some of those other divas?"

"Not at all. She's surprisingly down to earth. You should've seen how shook up she was yesterday. Those savages were all over her."

"Good thing you were there," his partner teased, elbowing him in the ribs.

"I know, right?" Mike replied, appalled by what he had witnessed that day.

"So, when are you going to see her again?" Ramirez asked, with a knowing look.

"I hadn't really thought about it. Her assistant came by this afternoon and invited me to dinner this weekend, but I don't know if I'm going."

"Came by the precinct? You're kidding right?"

"No. I guess she just wants to thank me," Mike said with a shrug.

"So let her thank you, man! Do you know how many guys—not just locally, or nationally, but *internationally*—would love to be in your shoes right now?! You'd have to be crazy not to go!"

"Ramirez, you have to see how that girl's living. She's way out of my league."

"She's still in the human league though, right?"

Mike chuckled. "Yeah, last time I checked."

Chapter 2

Mike was uncharacteristically anxious the Saturday evening he was scheduled to dine with Destiny; there was an odd feeling in the pit of his stomach. He chalked it up to nerves, changed his outfit three times and flossed his teeth twice, even though he hadn't eaten a bite the entire day. Finally, he settled on a pair of cedar brown pants, comfortable shoes and a knit shirt that had a subtle dark brown, teal and pale aqua print. It was a Christmas present from his younger sister—the family's resident fashionista—he'd never worn it because he thought it was too dressy. This seemed like the perfect occasion for it and he was satisfied with his appearance when he did a final once-over in his bedroom mirror. He put on his distressed leather bomber, grabbed his keys and walked out the door…

Destiny, in the meantime, was the picture of serenity.

Her hair stylist and makeup girl had just left and the restaurant she had ordered from had cooked dinner, delivered it, set it up and left shortly afterwards. Everything was perfect and looked as though she had spent hours preparing it. She wanted Officer Reilly to be impressed. After all, it wasn't every day that she invited a date over for dinner at her place. This night had to be perfect!

The telephone rang and she ran to grab it. It was building security informing her that her guest was on his way up. Destiny thanked the security guard and ran to take one last peek at herself in an antique cheval mirror. Her hair, makeup and outfit were stunning. She could hardly wait to see the cop's reaction!

With sudden butterflies in her stomach, Destiny raced over to the front door and flung it open. She knew that it was tacky, but she didn't care. She watched as Mike stepped off the elevator and then sighed like a school kid with her first crush. He was finer than she remembered.

It was going to be a great night.

"So, what's life like for an international recording star?" Mike asked, trying not to ogle Destiny as she reached into a cabinet to grab some fancy glassware.

"Busy," she replied with a hint of a smile. She'd caught him looking peripherally. The navy sarong ensemble with gold thread and beading really complimented her hair and complexion; she was more than aware of how good she looked. "I originally signed on as an R&B artist—the label hadn't expected me to cross over—but a couple of remixes on my latest CD did really well on the dance and pop charts, especially overseas. So life's been a lot busier and hectic than usual."

"So you're a victim of your own success," he observed, pouring iced tea into their glasses, as she hunted through a drawer for additional serving utensils.

"What do you mean?" she asked, pausing.

"Well, now you're so famous that you can't even go out to eat in public without being pounced on. Doesn't it drive you crazy?"

"Sometimes," she admitted with a little shrug, hoping that her lifestyle didn't turn him off because she was seriously digging Officer Reilly.

"I suppose that's the price you have to pay."

"Something like that," Destiny agreed, reaching for salad tongs. "So, tell me something about yourself."

"What would you like to know?" Mike asked.

"What made you decide to become a cop—you know— *stuff*. Humor me, Officer Reilly."

"Alright. My great grandfather was in law enforcement, my grandfather, my dad, and finally yours truly."

"Okay, fourth-generation policeman, did you do it because they pressured you to follow in their footsteps, or because you really do love the job?"

"Definitely the latter. My mother wanted me to be a doctor. I'm the oldest of three kids—I've got a brother who actually did go to med school and a sister who teaches at an elementary school."

"Any nieces, nephews?"

"Not yet, although our parents are definitely itching for a

few. How about you? Your turn to tell me something personal."

"Well, there's really not that much to tell. I'm an only child. My parents are well educated and quite successful in their respective careers. Not necessarily happy about *my* career choice—but, that's another story. They live overseas and I'm here in the States, so that helps. I had a healthy, happy childhood and didn't even start taking a serious interest in singing until I got to junior high and joined a glee club."

"Did success come easily for you?" he asked out of curiosity, spearing a cherry tomato covered in a fragrant balsamic vinaigrette.

"Strangely, yes. There weren't years of struggle, odd jobs and waiting for that 'big break.' A talent scout and his wife went to see their son perform in a college production of *West Side Story* and yours truly had been cast as the female lead. The rest is history. I'm a college drop-out, by the way. I try not to advertise it."

There was a comfortable silence as Mike processed all of that interesting information.

"Would you like coffee or tea with dessert?" she asked politely.

"Coffee, please." They were having red velvet cake sprinkled with white chocolate shavings; tea was not even an option, in his opinion.

"Do you believe in love at first sight, Officer Reilly?" she asked, as she handed him cream and sugar.

The question came from out of left field. Mike wondered momentarily what had prompted it. He decided to humor her. "I believe anything is possible. Here's to love," he replied, lightly tapping his glass against hers.

"To love," she echoed.

***

"Thank you for a very pleasant evening, Officer Reilly," she said, as they walked towards the front door of her condo.

"You're welcome. Thank you for inviting me. The food was excellent, by the way—give my compliments to the restaurant that prepared it," he smiled and she sighed inwardly.

"How'd you know I didn't make it?"

"I spotted one of the delivery bags behind your garbage can."

"You *are* good, officer! I thought I'd gotten rid of all the evidence. Does this mean you'll be taking me in?" she flirted, offering him her wrists.

Mike stared at her momentarily, thinking there were a lot of ways one could go with a remark like that. He decided to take the high road. "It's late. I'd better be heading out."

Destiny was impressed...he certainly wasn't easy. "May I see you again, Mike?"

"I don't know. I'll have my personal assistant contact you."

They both laughed. Chelsea was a gem and Destiny couldn't imagine life without her. "Well, I'm going to be in town for a little while and would really like to get together again."

"How about in two weeks?" he asked, turning the doorknob. "I'll cook."

"How about *tomorrow* and we let another restaurant do the cooking?" she suggested.

Mike tried not to laugh—she was something else—but he had really enjoyed her company. He kissed the back of her hand and pulled the front door open.

"Two weeks," he said firmly. "My place. I'll pick you up at seven."

"So, how'd it go?" Chelsea asked, handing Destiny a stack of fan mail when she stopped by later that evening.

"I think I'm in love!" she squealed, throwing the mail up into the air and dancing on top of it.

"Okay, who are you and what have you done with the singer?"

"Chelsea, I had such a great time!" she beamed, grabbing her assistant's hands.

"Please don't tell me that you slept with him."

"What? No way! This guy is the ultimate gentleman. He gave me a kiss on the back of my hand at the end of the night! Can you believe it? *My hand*! I didn't know if I should be insulted or curtsy!"

"You sure he's straight?"

"Positive."

"When are you seeing him again and am I going to have to make another trip down to his precinct?"

"Two weeks and no—he's coming to get me this time," she replied, doing a hip-hop step and humming her latest dance tune.

"Pretty flowers," Chelsea said, noticing the lovely arrangement in a crystal vase.

"Aren't they? He's so old school—I love it! Would you believe that he didn't even know that calla lilies are my favorites?"

"He might've looked it up on your web site."

"Nope. I wasn't getting that vibe from him. He looked genuinely surprised when I told him."

"Nice."

"Yeah," Destiny said dreamily. "He's a sweetie."

Chelsea helped clear the dining room table and then helped herself to some of the leftovers. She noticed that Destiny had used the Mikasa glasses; the pricey gem-colored ones that sparkled behind the doors of a curio, but never actually got used. She must've really wanted to impress him.

At least this one was a policeman. Hopefully that meant something.

Along with Destiny's fame came the downside of celebrity: too often her personal life made headline news. She usually dated people in the music industry, but once she had dated an 'A-lister' in the movie business and things had ended badly. It took months for the buzz to die down. Not that it had hurt Destiny's career. It seemed that with each public appearance, each consecutive award, and unfortunately, each new romance, the public's appetite for information about Destiny's personal life increased. Chelsea was glad that the cop appeared to have some values. It would be a nice change of pace from the self-absorbed actors, rich playboys and singers who usually pursued the chanteuse. Her world was like a Red Carpet circus, but apparently a necessary game for a rising star to play.

Chapter 3

"Ever been to one of these things before?" Chelsea asked the cop. They were on the set of Destiny's latest video shoot and Mike seemed so at ease that one might think he hung out backstage every day. He was wearing a pair of Old Navy boot cut jeans and a black knit shirt that would've put a Versace model to shame.

"No," Mike replied, his aquamarine eyes scanning the area for would-be offenders out of habit. "But I've seen enough of them on cable."

Chelsea chuckled, she liked him. He was so candid and unpretentious. The tabloids certainly loved him. He and Destiny had been seeing each other for quite a few weeks already and the press couldn't get enough. Now here he was at her latest video shoot. It'd probably be in some search engine's "trending" menu before the end of the day...

It was controlled chaos on the set. Sound and lighting technicians were scurrying about, a director was barking last-minute instructions, a choreographer was working with a couple of dancers over in another area, but there was no sign of the main attraction. Before Mike could ask Chelsea where her boss was, the lighting dimmed, music was queued, and Destiny and a light mist magically appeared center stage.

His breath caught, as he watched her. A stylist had crimped her waist-length tresses and everything from her eye shadow to her lip gloss shimmered with Urban Decay microglitter.

She really was something to behold.

Later on, Mike would recall that Destiny had been wearing some flesh-colored number strewn with Swarovski crystals and matching stilettos, but the thing that stayed with him was her voice...it blew him away. This wasn't some pop wannabe fresh off the assembly line. This woman really had a gift. And though the visuals were impressive, it was her talent that was unsurpassed...

"So, what did you think?" Destiny asked eagerly, glitter still sparkling on her skin. She had changed back into her street clothes, twisted her hair into a messy top knot, and she still looked awesome.

"I think those other R&B divas had better watch their backs," Mike teased, as she snuggled up against him.

"Thanks. But I was actually talking about the video. I don't know about that last bit of choreography…"

"You *really* want to know what I think?"

"Yes, I do."

Mike tilted her chin upwards and kissed her, letting her know what he thought without uttering a word.

Destiny trembled with pleasure. Sinking into the warmth of his strong frame, she allowed Mike to take the lead. He was appealing on so many levels and everything that she had ever hoped for…but was it real, or just an act? Too many before him had only been interested in her because of her looks, fame, or wealth. Destiny was not in the mood to play games, because it would be far too easy to fall in love with Officer Reilly. Far too easy…she worried, as the limo pulled up in front of her building and the kiss abruptly ended.

"Would you like to come upstairs?" she asked softly, with hopeful eyes.

"I've got to be at work early," he said shaking his head.

The driver was holding the door open for her and one of the security personnel was waiting to escort her inside the building.

"I guess this is goodnight, then."

"I'll call you tomorrow," he promised.

"I don't know if I can wait that long," she pouted.

Mike smiled. "You'll be fine. Go inside, it's chilly out there."

Destiny kissed him lightly on the cheek. "Thanks for tagging along."

"It was fun. Thanks for the invite."

"Sam, would you please take Officer Reilly home?" she graciously asked her limo driver.

The driver nodded and closed the passenger door. Mike gave him instructions to his apartment in Queens and then looked back through the tinted window. Destiny was still standing outside with the security guard. She was so rebellious. Didn't she realize it wasn't safe for her to do things like that? A smile slowly lit up Mike's expression. She would go inside once the limo was out of sight.

Destiny Jordan was crazy about him.

Chapter 4

"Come on!" Destiny grinned, grabbing Mike's hand.

"Where are we going?" he asked indulgently.

"I want to go grocery shopping," she announced one Thursday night, as though it were something she did every day.

"Not a good idea."

"Mike, don't be such a drag."

"I'm not being a drag, I'm using common sense. Don't you usually have your groceries delivered or picked up by Chelsea?"

"Yes, but I *need* some fresh air!"

"So go down to the lobby."

"You're worse than my last bodyguard!" she pouted.

"Glad to hear it," he said, turning on her laptop. "Here you go, order away."

"No. I'm going out...with or without you," she said defiantly, slipping on a newsboy cap and big sunglasses.

Mike shook his head. "Yeah, that's real subtle. I'm sure no one will recognize you."

The D'Agostino supermarket on 80th Street and York Avenue wasn't exactly empty when they went in, but at that time of evening at least the nine-to-five crowd was no longer an issue.

Mike breathed a sigh of relief as he and Destiny made their way up and down the aisles unmolested. He'd convinced her to lose the sunglasses and pin her hair up under the newsboy cap. Plain jeans and a nondescript jacket also played a role in disguising the star. There wasn't anything he could do to play down her gorgeous face; he hoped the brim of the oversized cap would help in that area.

"Mmm," she said, snagging a carton of fresh cherries and popping one into her mouth. "I love these...here, try one."

Mike was about to take the fruit from her hand, when she placed it against his lips. Before he knew what happened, they were kissing in the produce aisle, and her cap was on the floor.

A fan who secretly recorded the incident on a smart phone

uploaded the video to YouTube. Within minutes it went viral and over a million people witnessed Destiny's supermarket kiss.

***

"You know, there is a reason you pay me the big bucks," Chelsea drawled, as she turned the television off. "Why didn't you just let TMZ know what you were up to?"

"I was not going to call you back over here to go grocery shopping for me."

"Since when?"

"Since super cop arrived on the scene!" Destiny grinned.

"Cute. Real cute. Going forward, please refrain from such reckless behavior. I hate to break it to you, but you're an international recording star and there are too many nut jobs out there who would like to get their paws on you!"

"Aye aye, captain!"

Chelsea ignored her sarcasm. "Can we get down to business now?"

"If we must," Destiny said magnanimously.

"Dancing With The Stars. Interested or not?" she asked, flipping through a note pad.

"Oh, I love that show! Would I have time to squeeze it in? You think I can request Val for my pro partner? I would love for that man to teach me how to rumba!"

Chelsea held up a hand to stop the barrage of excited questions. "Not this year. You've got the new CD, photo and video shoots, awards shows, cosmetic endorsements, a new perfume, possibly a world tour next year—girlfriend, your plate is beyond full! And I'm not even going to answer that last question."

Destiny sighed.

"Maybe next season, girlfriend."

"Okay. What's next?"

"The talk show circuit—let's promote that new CD!"

"All right. Let's do Wendy Williams, The Real and Ellen DeGeneres."

"Done! See how easy all of this is when you sit down and focus?"

Destiny's cell phone suddenly rang. She checked the

caller ID and gave Chelsea a quick, apologetic look. "It's Mike."

"Go. I'm headed online to see what your fans are saying about the latest single and to chat with our favorite PR rep."

"You're the best!" Destiny grinned as she raced into her bedroom for some privacy.

"Yup. That's why I get paid the big bucks," Chelsea reiterated, as she logged on and began to review Destiny's fan page.

Chapter 5

Destiny and Mike were spending a relaxing Saturday afternoon together when he dared to ask her a question about her music. "Have you ever considered singing different types of songs?" Mike asked, as he installed her new 60-inch HD television.

Destiny frowned and folded her arms across her chest. "Like what—contemporary country?"

"No, I was thinking along the lines of inspirational or gospel. You've certainly got the voice for it. Besides, there's nothing wrong with songs that'll encourage or inspire people."

"What's wrong with songs that make them want to dance?"

"Nothing…it's just that your songs make them want to have sex, too," he replied while adjusting a couple of wires in the back of the set.

"It's just an image, Mike. Something the label creates based on what they believe the public wants."

"What do *you* want?"

"I just want to sing," she said. "The rest of it's not important."

"It should be important. It takes some people a lifetime to achieve your level of success and some never realize their dreams."

"So what are you saying, Officer Reilly?"

"Everything you are and have…it's all a gift from God. You didn't get where you are today by accident. Never forget who gave it all to you—"

"And who can take it all away?" she interjected.

"I was going to say just be mindful of what you're putting out there. Young girls and women are watching and imitating you; be one of the few that's a positive influence."

Destiny wanted to change the subject. No one ever confronted her about her music and she wasn't sure how to respond to Mike's comments. Sure, there was always some disgruntled parent somewhere griping about one of her videos or the lyrics, but she considered herself tame compared to some of the little pop tarts that were out there.

"Look, I know that sex sells and what you do with your career is your business, but I wouldn't say anything if I didn't care."

"*Why* do you care?" she asked solemnly. Nobody else did as long as their bank accounts remained fat.

Mike gazed down at her, resisted the urge to kiss her and then gently brushed his knuckles across her cheek. "Because you've got so much more to offer…now pass me the remote."

***

"What did you expect, Destiny?" Chelsea said. "The guy's got values. Personally, I think he's just what you need."

"You do, huh?"

"Yep. He's a far cry from the stuff you've dated in the past. I hope you don't scare him off."

Destiny threw a pillow at her assistant. "Why do I talk to you?"

"Because you need a conscience."

"No, I don't!"

"Yes, you do. If you'd had your way that cop would've been having breakfast in bed on your first date!"

"What's wrong with that?"

"Well, I'd like to think that *somebody* tried to instill some morals in you! Didn't you tell me once that your grandmother used to take you to church?"

"Dragged me is more like it—may she rest in peace. Why is church so much fun when you're a little kid and so boring when you're older?"

"I don't know, but a little Jesus in *your* life certainly wouldn't hurt!"

"Oh, not you, too! Haven't I heard enough sermons for one day?"

"Apparently not. You're only going to dinner a few avenues away, is it necessary to give the guy a coronary?" Chelsea asked, tipping her head towards the outfit hanging on the mirrored closet door. It was a form-fitting, bronze Nicole Miller slip dress with metallic threading that Destiny had bought just because of what it did for her eyes. She planned on wearing it with her floor-length Louis Féraud mink and a stunning pair of chandelier earrings she'd purchased while vacationing in Paris last year.

"If he does have an attack, I promise to give him the kiss of life," Destiny winked, perusing her wardrobe of evening shoes. She still couldn't decide between her favorite Jimmy Choo's or a new pair of Christian Louboutin's. "By the way, what time is my makeup girl coming?"

"In five, so chill. She'll be here," Chelsea said, handing her the metallic Jimmy Choo heels. "Word of advice?"

Destiny blew air between her teeth and stared intently at her assistant.

"Relax and be yourself; this isn't a press conference. I'd bet 10 to 1 that if you wore a pair of jeans and a tee shirt it wouldn't matter to Mike. There's not a shallow bone in that man's body."

"I know—he's such a treat! Still, you never know who might snap a picture. I'm not ending up on anybody's 'worst dressed' list! Besides, there's nothing wrong with leaving him panting for more."

"Well, I hope there's plenty of water on the table!" Chelsea replied shaking her head.

***

Destiny and Mike arrived at her favorite restaurant at exactly eight o'clock. A line of shivering people hoping to gain entrance had already formed outside, but the concierge temporarily ignored them. He immediately welcomed the recording star and her guest inside and notified the house that a VIP had just arrived.

As packed as the place was, Destiny and Mike were promptly escorted to a section reserved exclusively for VIP's and seated in a cozy, candlelit booth.

Celebrity membership certainly had its privileges.

Mike was constantly amazed at how people went out of their way to please Destiny. He wondered if he could ever get used to her lifestyle. It was still weird to him having to take a limo everywhere, when he owned a brand new SUV and was more than capable of protecting his date.

He watched Destiny as she placed her order and joked with the head waiter.

She was positively breathtaking that evening and the soft glow of the candlelight only accentuated the fact.

When they were finally alone, Mike laced his fingers through hers and their eyes met. It was going to be another magical evening and though there would probably be a swarm of photographers waiting to pounce on them the minute they went outside, it no longer seemed important.

Chapter 6

"Man, she's got you twisted!" Ramirez laughed.

"What?" Mike asked with a blank expression.

"I was talking to you about season tickets and you just zoned out!"

"Sorry, Ramirez," Mike said, running his fingers through his hair.

"It's okay, man. Just try to save the daydreaming for home, not while you're on the job!"

Mike nodded his head solemnly.

They were pulling into the precinct's parking lot. Thank God they didn't have a suspect in the backseat. He wouldn't have remembered what they'd arrested him for! In fact, he couldn't remember what they had done in the past hour. It was all a blur.

All he could think about was Destiny.

Ramirez was gesturing. He had just asked Mike something. "What?"

His partner was kind enough to repeat himself. "I was asking if you wanted to grab a bite to eat later."

It had been ages since he'd hung out with Ramirez after work. Lately, his world seemed to revolve around Destiny and that wasn't a good thing. Mike looked at his partner and grinned. "Sure, Ramirez. Why not?"

"You're like a lovesick teenager, Reilly! It's like you've got stardust in your eyes or something!" Ramirez chuckled. He took a sip of beer and reached for more overloaded nachos.

"I don't know what it is about this one," Mike said, his eyes staring blankly at a flat screen on a wall over the bar.

"First time in love, huh?"

"Guess so. I eat, sleep and drink that girl."

"More eating and drinking than sleeping...right?" Ramirez knew that Mike was a born-again Christian. He wondered if Destiny knew it. It struck him as odd that he hadn't heard Mike mention much about church or God in the past few months.

Usually, his partner couldn't shut up about God.

"I haven't laid a finger on her, if that's where you're headed with this."

"And you're *still* this whipped? Amazing!"

"It's not funny, Ramirez."

"I'm just happy to see you dating. Period."

"Yeah, I guess you would be after that last fiasco you set me up with!" Mike scoffed recalling a blind date he'd been on a few months ago.

"Look, I told you her English wasn't very good—at least she was cute! You should see some of the blind dates that I've gone out with!" Ramirez said with a shudder.

Mike was laughing until he glanced back at the television. A commercial advertising a sneak peek of Destiny's latest music video was on; it seemed as though every guy in the sports bar simultaneously stopped talking.

Ramirez turned around to see what had captured everyone's attention. He looked back at Mike and shook his head. "I feel for you, partner. I really do."

***

Mike raced over to Destiny's place as soon as he left the sports bar. He couldn't stand being without her for another minute. He knew that she'd had a busy day—something about photo shoots and a CoverGirl commercial—but he couldn't go home without seeing her…especially after that video.

When he arrived, he blew right past the doormen and made a bee line for the security console. The guards were already familiar with him, but they still called Destiny to confirm that it was okay for him to go upstairs.

When the elevator doors opened, she was waiting to greet him with opened arms. "Hey," she said, squeezing him tightly. "I missed you today."

Mike was speechless. He held her close and kissed her. His heart was so full, he couldn't even begin to explain it. He never wanted to let her go.

"Chelsea said that you must be a saint," Destiny said, as she sipped an excellent California zinfandel.

"Doing my best," he assured her, his head resting on her lap.

"So, you do go to church?"

"Yes and I'm a youth leader."

"What's a youth leader and how come you never mentioned it before?" she asked, her hands stilling from stroking his hair.

"It just never came up in conversation, to answer your second question. As for the first one: at my church a youth leader is a person in the ministry who meets once a week with the teens or young adults, usually on a Friday night. We pray, eat, talk about the things that concern them and much more."

"It sounds like a huge responsibility," she replied, her respect for Mike increasing ten-fold.

"It is and I don't take it lightly."

"Does your church pay you for your services?"

"No. I'm a volunteer."

"Wow…"

"Hey, why don't you go with me next Friday night and check it out?"

"I don't know, Mike…"

"You're not afraid of a few high school kids," he teased.

"Absolutely not—they buy a good percentage of my CDs!"

"Okay, then it's a date."

"To Friday night, Officer Reilly," Destiny said, gazing into the crackling flames of the fireplace.

***

There were about 25 of them and the only thing they seemed to have in common was their joy at seeing Mike. A couple of the girls actually ran up to him and gave him hugs. Destiny was pleased to note that their upper bodies didn't make full contact. The young people gathered together in a circle, held hands and Mike opened the meeting with prayer. Afterwards there was a bit of a hustle as everyone went over to a refreshment table and rounded up snacks and beverages.

"Everyone, this is Destiny," Mike said after they had all found a seat at two adjoining banquet tables and the chatter had finally died down. The group turned to look at her in awed unison.

"Wow! You look younger in real life than you do in your videos," one teen blurted. "Are you going to sing for us?"

"Karen!" another teen hissed, rolling her eyes to the ceiling. "Please forgive her, Miz Destiny, she ain't housebroke yet!"

Destiny was grateful for her thick skin. A few years in the industry limelight had taught her how to smile graciously and not get offended by the public's insensitive, running commentary. She had definitely heard worse. She gave the group her warmest smile and patted the embarrassed teen gently on her hand. "Thanks for the compliment, Karen. You'd be amazed at what my makeup girl can do!"

Everyone started laughing, easing the tension, but Mike gave the first teen a censuring look. "Destiny's not here to sing. She's my special guest this evening and we are not going to ask her any more embarrassing questions *or* to sing. Is that clear?"

"Um, Mike?" Destiny carefully interjected with a slightly raised hand.

"Yes?"

"I wouldn't mind singing for the youth group."

The teens roared their approval. It took five minutes to calm them down.

Mike had his reservations, though. He knew a couple of the songs that Destiny was famous for and *none* of the lyrics were appropriate for this venue. He looked at her uncertainly.

Destiny gave him a reassuring smile. She had so many tricks up her sleeve—Officer Reilly had no idea. She stood up, closed her eyes and began to belt out a song called *Sing For Me*, which she'd heard playing on the radio years ago and fallen instantly in love with. When she finished there wasn't a dry eye in the place and the applause was so heartfelt that she had to blink back tears of her own.

"You didn't have to do that, you know," Mike said quietly,

but the gratitude in his eyes belied his words.

"I know, but I wanted to," she said sincerely.

"Well, thanks. I'm pretty sure that Friday nights will never be the same again!"

"I'm glad I went."

"I'm glad you did, too."

"What now?" she asked, as he escorted her inside her building.

Mike nodded at the security guards at the console. "You go upstairs and get some rest."

"Alone?"

"Afraid so."

"Still playing hard to get, Officer Reilly?" she teased, as she pressed the elevator button.

"No. Just being a gentleman. Your ride's here," he said kissing her on the cheek.

Destiny sighed and watched him until the elevator doors closed.

Just her luck, was what it was. Only *she* would find herself a super fine boyfriend who happened to be a born-again Christian. Her grandmother would have been thrilled.

Too bad Destiny wasn't.

Chapter 7

Mike was doing his favorite thing one quiet Saturday evening: spending quality time with Destiny. No flashing cameras, screaming fans, or limo rides to places he had to dress up for. They had just finished watching a movie on TBN and Destiny was practically bursting at the seams with questions. She could hardly wait until the credits started rolling.

"I don't get it—I mean, I believe in God and the Bible, but there are so many do's and don'ts! It's like God's this great big cop in the clouds just waiting to bop you over the head with a night stick and put you on the hell express the minute you mess up! How can you live like that?"

Mike refrained from laughing out loud. It wasn't often that he and Destiny had conversations of a spiritual nature, so he had to tread carefully and laughing wasn't an option.

"First of all, the last thing God wants to do is put you on the 'hell express'—He'd rather have you spend eternity in Heaven with Him. Secondly, if you really understood how much He loves and cares about you, you'd realize that those so-called do's and don'ts are for your own protection. God wants what's best for us all the time and if it takes writing it in stone or in a book to get our attention, well, that's what He'll do."

"It's just not a *fun* way to live," Destiny pouted, wrapping her arms around Mike's waist and gazing up at him impishly.

"Life's not always about *fun*, Destiny. There are a whole lot of people out there—wealthy, beautiful, who seem to have it going on. People who passionately pursue things to make them happy and you know what? Most of them aren't. In fact, the more things some people have the more miserable they seem to be. And the more *fun* some of them have the more trouble they seem to get into. Just a thought."

"Gosh—" Destiny said with wonder.

"What?"

"Are you always this uptight?"

Mike chuckled softly. "I'm a youth leader *and* a cop."

"Well, I for one think that you need to loosen up a bit."

"That's what the gym's for," he replied with a sparkle in his eyes.

"You absolutely, positively fascinate me!"

"Why?" he asked, nonplussed.

"You're so…moral."

"Is that such a bad thing?"

"It could be. Just seems like you're setting yourself up for a fall. Nobody's perfect and everybody has weaknesses."

"That's why we pray," Mike said with a smile.

"So what'll it take to get you in bed, Officer Reilly?" she asked, abruptly changing gears. It annoyed her that they were not intimate and she was completely baffled by his ability to resist her.

Mike didn't immediately respond. Destiny had no idea how often he prayed for strength to keep his hands off her. He lived his life according to the Bible's standards and that meant no premarital sex. No exceptions. Although he couldn't remember ever wanting a woman so badly. Of course, there were very few women who looked the way she did. "It'll take marriage, Destiny. I'm not a casual sex kind of guy."

"So, let's get married," she said, without missing a beat.

Mike blinked. "Are you for real? You'd marry someone just to sleep with them?"

"Oh, my gosh—just kidding!" she teased rolling her eyes. "But, just for the record, *sleeping* wasn't exactly what I had in mind."

Mike's aquamarine eyes bored through her. "We hardly know each other—"

"We've been dating for *months*! Live a little, Mike!" she exclaimed, throwing her arms around his neck.

Mike gently removed them. Things had been steaming up between them lately and even the innocent kisses were evolving into more. He understood that she had needs—he did, too—but compromise was out of the question. "This is crazy. We shouldn't even be having this discussion."

"Why not? Aren't you attracted to me?" Mike's playing

hard to get was getting under Destiny's skin in more ways than one. He acted like God didn't know they had libidos! Who did he think invented them?

"A man would have to be dead to not be attracted to you, Destiny. But there's more to a relationship than looks. The woman I marry has to be saved."

"I used to go to church when I was a kid, doesn't that count?" she joked.

"No. You have to have a personal relationship with Jesus Christ *now*, or the marriage will never work."

"So convert me!" she said dramatically.

"This isn't a game, Destiny."

"Okay, then tell me something: if your relationship with God is so important to you and it matters so much who you hook up with, then what are you doing with me?"

Mike stared at her. He was at a loss for words. He wasn't going to tell her that she was all he thought about, or how distracted he was at work, which was never a good thing in his field. He lived and breathed for the moments they shared.

He'd had his share of pretty girlfriends, crushes, and women who had pursued him over the years, but he'd never experienced anything like this. Destiny was the love of his life.

"I think it's time to call it a night," he said solemnly, standing up. Destiny's question had struck a nerve and he suddenly felt uneasy.

"Don't go. I hate it when you leave," she said softly, taking him by the hand.

He slowly sat back down on the floral-print settee, his expression troubled.

"What is it?" she asked. "I promise, I'll still respect you in the morning!" she teased, trying to lighten the mood. But Mike wasn't bighting.

"Don't ever kid around about us getting physical."

"I'm sorry. Sometimes I forget that's a sensitive area for you. Will you forgive me?"

"Of course I will, but you need to understand something," he said staring into her eyes. "We've got more against us than for

36

us and I don't like not knowing where this is going."

"Why does it have to be going anywhere?" she asked with a frown.

"I wake up and I'm thinking about you, I go to sleep and I'm thinking about you—this isn't just some fling for me."

"It's not for me either…I'm in love with you."

Mike inhaled slowly. *"What?"*

"You heard me. I've never met anyone who wasn't bowled over by who I am, what I have, or what they thought I could do for them. None of this crap fazes you. You're so real and more importantly, I feel safe with you. Safer than I've felt in a really long time." Embarrassed, Destiny glanced away blinking rapidly. "I don't know why I'm so emotional tonight. You must think I'm crazy."

"No, I don't and just for the record…the feeling's mutual," he said, placing a kiss on her temple.

"So what are we going to do about it?"

"I don't know, Destiny. I really don't know."

Chapter 8

Mike picked up his Bible and it fell open to 1 Corinthians 6:18.

Flee fornication…

He felt a chill go through him. He'd seen that scripture before and he'd been hearing those exact words in his spirit for days. He looked at the rest of the scripture. *Every sin that a man doeth is without the body; but he that committeth fornication sinneth against his own body.*

He immediately dropped to his knees and prayed for forgiveness and strength. He knew that the Bible said he wouldn't be tested beyond what he was able to handle, but his involvement with Destiny was pushing him dangerously close to the brink.

Sin lieth at the door.

He knew that one. It was in the book of Genesis—right before Cain killed Abel…

***

Mike made an appointment to meet with his pastor the very next day.

He had been a member of Living Waters Christian Center since his early twenties and loved his church and pastor. His work partner, Ramirez, was great with advice about women, but Mike knew there was only one person he could trust when it came to safeguarding his soul.

"Mike, it's good to see you. Please, make yourself comfortable," the pastor said with a warm smile.

"Thanks for seeing me on such short notice, Pastor Hammond," Mike said gratefully, settling into a worn, but comfortable dark brown leather chair in the office.

"Your voicemail message sounded pretty urgent."

"It is."

"Well, then, let's pray!"

After the two men had prayed, Mike filled his pastor in on what had recently taken place in his life.

"What are you doing with her?" the pastor asked bluntly.

"Just dating her," Mike quickly replied.

"That wasn't what I meant when I asked that question, Mike."

"Oh," he said, feeling like an idiot.

"The Word of God says in 2 Corinthians 6:14: *Be ye not unequally yoked together with unbelievers: for what fellowship hath righteousness with unrighteousness? And what communion hath light with darkness?* You had no business 'just dating' her in the first place."

"Pastor, do you know *who* I'm talking about?" Mike asked.

"It doesn't matter. I know the Bible has plenty of stories about men who were brought low by a pretty face. Remember Samson?"

"But, I love her."

"Since you've become involved with this woman, you're barely serving in the youth outreach ministry, haven't come out on prayer night, or been to Bible study in weeks. God should always be your first priority, Mike. Remember: He's a jealous God."

"So what are you saying, that I should just forget how I feel and walk away?" Mike asked with an exasperated expression.

"I'm saying that you should seek the Father's heart in this matter…your own can lead you astray."

***

Mike left his pastor's office frustrated and anxious. His pastor wasn't married or in love. How could he expect him to understand? Mike couldn't even imagine life without Destiny in it. He almost felt relieved when his cell phone rang and the caller ID showed that she was at the other end of the line.

"Hey," he said quietly.

"Hey, handsome! Whatcha up to?"

"Nothing much," he said as he climbed into his SUV and stared blindly out the window.

"Why don't you come over and watch a movie with me?"

"What kind of movie?"

"Any kind you like."

Mike felt a tingle of warning creep down his spine. He shook it off.

"What time?"

"Now."

"Shall I bring anything?"

Destiny laughed huskily. "Just yourself, Officer Reilly."

"I'll be right there."

"Wait…a…minute—" Mike said between kisses.

"No," Destiny breathed. "No more minutes…no more waiting."

He had to pin her hands above her head to get her attention.

"Nice trick. Do we get to play with the handcuffs now, Officer Reilly?" she laughed softly.

She was incorrigible and he was hopelessly addicted to her. Mike abruptly released her. How they had ended up on her bed after watching a DVD was a mystery to him. How she had ended up wearing nothing but her underwear was a bigger mystery. He refused to look at her, because just looking weakened his resolve. He had to get out of there before they both did something he was sure he'd end up having to repent for. Mike pulled his shirt back over his head, hoping that she would get the message.

This party was definitely over.

"Hey," she said softly, causing him to pause.

What was it about the way she said that particular word?

Ignoring his libido's response to her voice, Mike wordlessly handed her a silk robe. "Cover yourself."

Destiny flung the robe on the floor. "I bought this La Perla outfit just for you…you seemed to really like it twenty minutes ago. Please explain to me what happened between then and now!"

They had never gone this far before—that's what had happened—and it disturbed him how easily he lost control around her lately. "This isn't how it's supposed to be, Destiny."

"Well, please enlighten me—how is it *supposed to be*?" she almost shouted, wanting to punch him. He was the most moral, most complex man she'd ever known and it only made her want him more.

"Not like this. Not some quick roll in the hay with zero commitments. Don't you want more?"

"Right this second? No! What's the big deal?"

"I want more! That's the big deal!"

"More of what?! You already know that I love you!" she said in frustration.

"I feel as though you're not getting it."

"Not getting *what*?"

"Just hear me out. I have an idea."

"Why do I get the feeling that I'm not going to like this?"

"Come to church with me, Destiny."

"*What?!*"

"You need to understand why I believe what I believe. Besides, it's only fair. I go just about everywhere with you."

"How can you compare a video shoot or an awards show with *church*?" she asked with an incredulous expression.

"If you care anything us, about *me*, you'll at least think about it. I'm not asking for much."

Destiny remained silent. He *was* asking her for much, he just didn't realize it. She hadn't stepped foot inside a church since she was a kid. She gazed at Mike; he was an enigma to her, yet she was crazy about him. Still, she felt as though there was nothing she could deny him. She exhaled slowly and met his aquamarine gaze. "All right, Officer Reilly. I'll think about it."

Chapter 9

Destiny couldn't remember the last time she'd been so uncomfortable. She was wearing a knee-length, navy blue dress with a georgette overlay that Chelsea had bought for her because it was 'respectable,' matching sling-back silk heels, conservative jewelry and seriously toned-down makeup and she still felt like there was a spotlight on her.

Maybe if the congregation stopped staring for five minutes as they searched for seats she wouldn't feel so uptight. Then again, maybe she was just being a drama queen. To some of those people she was simply a new face that happened to be dating one of their youth leaders. She wouldn't allow herself to dwell on what the rest of the congregants might be thinking.

She sighed with relief when they finally located two seats, which were not too close to the pulpit and—thank God—situated at the end of the row (perfect for a quick getaway, if necessary). Destiny made a mental note to give Mike a huge kiss later on. He squeezed her hand reassuringly and waited until she sat down before he claimed his own seat.

Praise and worship, Destiny discovered, was a blast and the choir was excellent. She was actually enjoying the service, until the pastor started preaching about fornication. Destiny held her breath momentarily, hoping that the pastor wouldn't stay on the top for too long, but her wishing was in vain. It was almost as though that man of God could read her mind. By the time he finished reading the last scripture Destiny was ready to run from the building screaming. Mike had to tap her on the shoulder to get her attention.

"Are you okay? You look a little flushed," he noted with concern.

"Is it over?" she whispered.

"Yeah—about 10 minutes ago."

Destiny exhaled and braved a look around. People were filing down the aisles towards the exits. Some smiled shyly, a couple of teens from Mike's youth group waved excitedly, other people stared and one couple looked like they wanted to make the sign of the cross.

Hopefully that was just her imagination.

"Come on," Mike said taking her by the hand.

"Where are we going now?" she almost whined.

"I want you to meet my pastor," Mike said proudly.

Destiny could have crawled under one of the pews. Meeting the preacher was the last thing she wanted to do. "He looks busy," she said, noticing the line of people waiting to greet him.

"Trust me, he's never too busy to chat with one of the youth leaders."

"Okay, if you insist," she said sullenly.

"Chin up," Mike said chuckling. "If you think today's message was rough you should have heard last week's sermon on *offense*."

"That transparent, huh?" she asked feeling like a brat.

"A bit. Come on, it won't be so bad."

"Brother Mike!" the pastor bellowed warmly.

"Pastor Hammond," Mike replied respectfully, shaking the older man's hand.

"It's good to see you and I see that you've brought a guest," the pastor said.

"Pastor Hammond, this is Destiny," Mike said, pulling her gently from behind him.

"Hello, Destiny. It's nice to finally meet the young lady who's had our most dedicated youth leader so distracted."

Destiny was about to shake the pastor's hand, but her hand froze mid-air after his comment.

"Honey, he's just kidding," Mike lied.

Blushing furiously, Destiny allowed the pastor to shake her hand and to her surprise, when their eyes met, she did not see the censure she had expected, but gentleness and compassion.

"Thank you for fellowshipping with us today, Destiny. We hope that you'll worship with us again soon," the pastor said graciously.

"Thank you," she mumbled.

"Have a blessed day, Pastor," Mike said, as he ushered Destiny through an exit door. "Are you alright?"

"Yes, it was just a weird moment. I don't know what I was expecting him to say or do…"

"He doesn't bite, Destiny."

"I know, it's just that when he was in the pulpit preaching, it was like he was speaking directly to me."

"Trust me, you're not the only one," Mike said, remembering how some of the pastor's words had been like a sucker punch to his gut.

"Is it always like that?"

"Like what?"

"You know—straight, no chaser."

Mike almost laughed. "That's a funny way of putting it. My pastor never waters down the Word to make folks feel comfortable in their sin."

Destiny pondered those words.

She was comfortable in her sin…and she and God both knew it.

***

"So, how was church?" Chelsea asked with a neutral expression.

That was a loaded question. Destiny put on her best poker face and smiled angelically. "It was delightful. I even met the pastor."

Chelsea almost choked from laughing so hard.

Not exactly the reaction Destiny was expecting.

"You're not lying, right? I mean, you just got out of service. You'd at least wait until Monday to lie, wouldn't you?"

"I'm glad you think it's so funny," Destiny fumed.

"So how was it really?"

"It wasn't bad," Destiny insisted, anxiously reaching for her hairbrush.

Chelsea snatched it up before the chanteuse yanked out all of her platinum streaks. "Okay. What was the sermon about?"

"Fornication," Destiny said hoarsely. "I thought lightning was going to hit me and take out the entire pew."

"Why? Were you and Mike *not* the only ones breaking out in a cold sweat?"

"I just couldn't believe that the one time I get up the nerve to go to church with Mike is the day the pastor decides to cover that topic! Do you think Mike told him I was going to be visiting today?" Destiny asked, her cheeks blazing with indignation.

"No. I would hope that Mike and his pastor have better things to do with their time. It was just what my mama would've called a *word in season.*"

"What's *that* supposed to mean?"

"That means what you heard today wasn't a coincidence. That sermon—if it really got under your skin—was tailor-made for you...compliments of the Holy Spirit, Himself."

"Great. Give me another reason not to go back," Destiny said dejectedly. God sending her customized messages through a preacher was not her idea of a good time.

Chelsea got up from the kitchen table and gave Destiny's shoulder a reassuring squeeze. "You done good, girlfriend. I, for one, am proud of you."

Destiny smiled tremulously. "His church was actually nice; you should tag along one day."

"Now you know that if I don't go to my uncle's church when I'm in town my family will hunt me down!"

"I don't know, Chelsea. I saw a couple of good-looking deacons that might've had you shoutin' in the aisles!"

"Very funny. You keep showing up at God's house and you might have to eat those words."

"Speaking of eating—how about some Italian tonight?" Destiny asked, rooting through a drawer full of menus.

"Only if you're doing a salad. Your favorite D&G dress was fitting you like a glove on that talk show the other day."

Destiny grimaced. "I know. I swear that once you hit 30 everything you eat goes right to your—"

"I get the picture. What you need to do is cut out some of that late-night dining with super cop."

"He is pretty super, isn't he?" Destiny sighed, practically glowing.

"All he needs is the cape."

"Hey! You think Mike would be willing to go on a talk show with me?" Destiny mused.

"I think that pigs might fly first. Why don't you ask him?"

"I will, but, not on an empty stomach. Care to split some spinach lasagna and garlic knots with me?"

"As long as there's a side of tiramisu, I'm game."

"Good," Destiny said handing her the menu. "Then you can order."

Chapter 10

A whore is a deep ditch.

Mike heard those startling words as clearly in his mind as if someone standing beside him had spoken them aloud. Sighing heavily, he closed his Bible and waited patiently; he knew that more was coming.

How far do you plan on falling?

"I love her, Lord and I don't appreciate the name calling," Mike said defensively.

Check out the book of Proverbs and you'll see why I said that. Besides, I know that you love her, but is she worth burning for?

Mike burned for Destiny every night! Surely God knew that by now.

That's not the kind of burning I was referring to. You know what I mean. Is she worth spending an eternity in hell?

"No one and nothing is worth spending forever in hell, Lord."

Then why are you still pursuing her and allowing yourself to be tempted by her? Remember, Mike, obedience is better than sacrifice.

"I don't know what to do, Lord! I've tried to stay away from her, but it only makes me want her more!"

There's a way that seems right to a man, but the end is death. Don't allow her to be the cause of yours.

"If you didn't want us to be together, why did you allow me to meet Destiny in the first place? You knew that I would fall in love with her! Who wouldn't?"

One who keeps his eyes on me, was the gentle reply. *Destiny was a test sent by the enemy to ensnare you and so far you've been failing miserably.*

"What do you want me to do, Lord?"

Let her go.

Mike almost stopped breathing. He was hoping that God would say anything but that.

She's a broad path of pain and destruction for you.

"So you're saying she'll never be saved?" Mike whispered brokenly.

I'm saying it will be years before she's ready. I'm saying... this day...choose life instead of death.

***

Destiny stood outside Mike's front door gritting her teeth.

She hadn't seen or heard from him in two weeks! Not a phone call, text message, e-mail—nothing! How dare he ignore her phone calls and blow her off like she was some nobody who didn't mean a thing to him?! Like she couldn't pick up her cell phone and have a line of rich and famous men from every walk of life beating a path to her front door!

She was debating on how many pieces of her mind she was going to give to Officer Reilly when he finally decided to open the door. For the three minutes they simply stared at one another Destiny considered abandoning her tirade. She was just happy and relieved to see him; he looked so handsome standing there...handsome, resigned and uncertain. *Why was he looking uncertain?* Suddenly she was angry again.

"I see you still live at the same address," she announced pushing past him into his apartment. "Did you forget mine?"

"What are you doing here?" he asked.

"Excuse you?" she said, whirling around to face him. "I think I'm the only one who has a right to be asking any questions! For instance: did you dump me and conveniently forget to mention it?"

"You already know the answer to that."

"No, I don't. What's going on, Mike?"

"Nothing's going—"

"Stop lying!" Destiny shouted.

Mike exhaled slowly. The wounded look in her eyes was killing him. How could he make her understand that their relationship could destroy them both for an eternity? He reached out to hold her and she shook him off. She was a star that some men would give their right arm to be with...she'd never understand that this was for their own good.

48

"Do you realize what we almost did the other night, Destiny?" he asked.

"Is *that* what this is all about?!" she exclaimed with a frown. "If you knew you'd be beating yourself up about it later why didn't you just leave after we watched the DVD?"

"For the same reason I'm fighting to keep my hands off you now. I want you. Plain and simple. And every time we're together…I don't know if I'll have the strength to stop myself. That's why I've been keeping my distance. For the sake of both our souls."

Destiny was so tired of him. He was like that Katy Perry song: hot and then cold. She exhaled slowly and searched for words that would help him to understand things from a non-spiritual point of view. "Despite what the tabloids may imply, I'm very particular about who gets in my bed and who I trust with my heart. So please don't take that lightly, because I don't."

"Destiny, I don't take anything about you lightly," he replied.

"Then stop fighting whatever this is and just surrender to it."

"I wish it were that simple," he said shaking his head and turning his back to her.

"It is," she said coming up behind him. "You're the only one who's making it complicated."

He turned to face her and knew immediately that it was going to be another cold shower night. This had to be what King David felt like when he saw Bathsheba bathing from his rooftop.

Destiny's desire for Mike was evident in everything from her eyes to her body language and it was a powerful aphrodisiac which he battled constantly. Lately it was getting harder and harder to resist her. It had been a long time since he had been intimate with anyone and his body reminded him about it daily. If he had not been saved their relationship would have been consummated months ago.

He kissed Destiny on her forehead and abruptly released her. He was already over by the front door with his hand on the knob when she finally opened her startled eyes.

"Is your driver still waiting for you?"

"What was *that*?" she asked, ignoring his question.

"Please, let's just call it a night, Destiny."

"I don't think so!"

Catching him off guard, she wrapped her arms tightly around his neck and pressed her lips against his. Mike's first instinct was to stop her before things got out of hand again, but as the kiss progressed he found himself becoming the aggressor, until she breathlessly tore away.

"Now *that* was a kiss, Officer Reilly! My limo's outside. Sweet dreams," she said with a shaky triumphant smile.

It was one o'clock in the morning and Mike was still awake. Sometimes a cold shower helped, sometimes it didn't. Tonight it had been a waste of water thanks to Destiny and the lip lock they'd shared before she sashayed out his front door.

He had to break up with her...

Being with Destiny was like standing at the edge of a precipice waiting to bungee jump—there was the excitement, anticipation and adrenaline rush, but there was also danger. Getting a warning from God was no joke.

Destiny was trouble, with a capital T. She was the kind of temptation that men burned willingly for, the kind that caused empires to crumble...the kind that could make a man eat a piece of fruit and live to regret it for the rest of his mortal days.

And Mike wanted to taste that fruit.

Didn't want to go to hell for it, but he definitely wanted a taste.

Even though he knew in his gut that one taste would never satisfy him.

He had never been a one-night-stand sort of guy and if he cared enough about a woman to get physical then that meant he was interested in a long-term, monogamous relationship with her. Not a hit and run.

Lusting after a woman this way didn't make any sense. It dulled him spiritually and made him cranky and physically uncomfortable.

50

All he thought about lately was sex.

Mainly how long it had been and how badly he wanted it. Between X-rated dreams and impure thoughts about Destiny, he was losing control. Sometimes the dreams were so real that when he woke up he was shocked to find his bed empty.

If he stayed in bed, in the dark, he might begin fantasizing about her, so Mike switched on the lamp and turned on the television.

Destiny was staring back at him.

One of the cable channels was doing an encore presentation of an awards show she had recently performed at.

Groaning with frustration he watched helplessly as she and her infamous back-up dancers worked the stage and whipped the audience into a frenzy.

That was his woman.

How in the world had that happened?

Mike turned the television off.

He could lay there for hours torturing himself with thoughts of her, or he could do something to let off some steam. He got up and slipped his feet into his Nikes and grabbed his keys.

A late-night jog was just what the doctor ordered.

Chapter 11

"Brother Mike!" a young man with an unruly ponytail exclaimed as he ran up to Mike in the supermarket and gave him a fierce hug.

"Jesse! How's it going?" Mike asked, returning the hug. He'd known Jesse since junior high school and had seen firsthand how the power of God could transform a life. Mike was proud that he'd been instrumental in that conversion. Jesse had a rap sheet by the time he was sixteen and it was the youth program at Mike's church that had helped turn his life around before it was too late.

"It's going—you know—God's good all the time!"

"Yeah, man. That's the truth. How's your girlfriend doing?"

"You mean my fiancée—"

"Get out!" Mike exclaimed. "When's the big day?"

"June, next year."

"Congrats, man."

"Thanks, Brother Mike. I'm putting an invitation in the mail for you and a guest—feel free to bring any recording stars you may know. Hint, hint."

Mike looked at him sheepishly. "So you heard."

"Who hasn't heard? Should I be congratulating you?"

"More like you should be praying for me," Mike somberly replied.

"It's like that, huh?"

"She's not saved, Jesse. We're as unequally yoked as they come."

"You gotta watch that. The unsaved ones can drag you right back down into the pit with them."

"Don't I know it," Mike said running his fingers anxiously through his hair.

"Destiny's gorgeous, but I don't envy you."

"I wouldn't envy me either."

"How'd the two of you even meet?"

Mike smiled. "I'm still trying to figure that one out."

"I hear you. Sometimes your flesh just doesn't agree with your spirit—"

"Sometimes?"

"You got a point there. If it's any consolation I understand what you're going through."

"Yeah? So how'd yours turn out?"

"Mine got saved, remember? I ended up putting a ring on her finger."

"Congrats again on both counts."

"Thanks," the young man grinned momentarily, then looked earnestly at his mentor. "Try not to trip it, Brother Mike. God knew you were going to fall for her. Like you told me once: 'there's a reason for the season.' It's probably just a test."

"If it is I'm not doing too well," Mike admitted, grateful to finally be able to speak with someone who understood what he was going through.

"You're going to be okay," Jesse decided. "Just keep your eyes on Him."

"That's kind of hard right now, considering who I'm dating."

Jesse chuckled. "Like I said before: I don't envy you. But I do miss seeing you on Friday nights. Everyone does... especially that new kid, Karen."

"I know," Mike said guiltily. "I'll be back soon. I promise."

"Just remember: He's a jealous God. I'd better finish picking up the rest of the stuff on this grocery list for my aunt. Hope to see you again soon, Brother Mike."

"Likewise. Take care, Jesse," Mike murmured, as the young man disappeared down the produce aisle. That was the second time someone had said that to him about God and it chilled him to the bone.

Chapter 12

Destiny backed off for a few weeks and allowed Mike to pull himself back together. If she had known that getting frisky on her bed in some lacey underthings was going to have him tripping so much she would have done it sooner. She'd had a taste of just how passionate Officer Reilly could be that night and she wanted seconds. For now, he had made her a promise months ago and she was not letting him off the hook. He was just going to have to man up and work it out, because they were going to the American Music Awards, if she had to tie him up and drag him!

Surprisingly, when she finally called him about it, Mike didn't put up a fuss. He truly was a man of his word. Despite the fact that the AMA's were in Los Angeles and they would have to be traveling and staying at a hotel together…

Mike had convinced himself that he could handle it. He had promised Destiny that he would accompany her to this particular awards show and he wasn't going to leave her hanging on such an important night. Or give her the option of inviting someone else.

After all, they would be sleeping in separate rooms at the hotel and all he had to do was escort her to the show, maybe to an after-party and then they'd be back in New York, safe and sound. No hanging out in her room, no romantic candlelit dinners, no opening the door to temptation. Period. No big deal.

The night of the show, he glanced one more time in the mirror, adjusted his black tie and turned the light off in his room. He knocked on Destiny's door and felt his resolve slip in a major way when she opened it. Mike nearly choked as she spun around in a giddy circle.

"What do you think? It's a Dolce & Gabbana—they designed it just for me!"

It was a strapless, black lace confection with a nude underlining that showed off all of Destiny's assets. Mike felt like calling for backup. It felt sinful just looking at her. Everything about her appearance was designed to entice…from her waist-skimming, bone-straight mane, to her lace designer stilettos.

"You look incredible," he said hoarsely.

"So do you, Officer Reilly. Are you excited?"

"I'm excited for you. It's a big deal getting nominated for an American Music Award. Your stylist insisted that Armani was the way to go, so he gets all the credit. Is he straight, by the way?"

"What do you think?" she asked dryly.

"I was kind of hoping that he was just another metrosexual, but there was something about the way he kept admiring my shoulders."

"As long as he didn't try to put the moves on you—I'd really hate to fire his narrow behind!"

"Somehow he knows I'm off limits, so that won't be necessary."

The phone rang, interrupting their conversation. Destiny answered it and then hung up with a smile that bordered on contagious. "Our limo's downstairs. Shall we?" she asked, offering him her arm.

***

The Nokia Theater's Red Carpet was something to behold. Celebrities, their significant others, and their bodyguards arrived by the minute in limos, but none were as anticipated as Destiny and her policeman. Mike was patient with the inquisitive journalists thrusting microphones in their faces and the perfect arm accessory for the vocalist whom everyone knew was a shoo-in for at least a couple of the evening's AMA's. The fans and media loved him.

He sat expectantly, front and center, surrounded by celebrities from an interesting array of industries. Destiny was scheduled to perform in a few minutes and he was grateful that the show was coming to its conclusion. He had never seen so many indecent garments and outlandish performances in his life. Mike had grown up when videos were more about promoting the music and was fully aware of just how bad things had gotten. Anything went these days. That's why he found some of Destiny's videos so scandalous. Singers without real vocals had to use their physical assets to gain popularity. Stars like Destiny didn't…yet she chose to. He would never understand that.

The house lights darkened and the audience was allowed the pure pleasure of hearing Destiny's voice before they actually saw her. Mike unconsciously clutched the armrests of his seat. Her voice was blowing right through him again; melodious, beguiling, compelling. He felt his heartbeat accelerate as a spotlight encompassed her. She was wearing that same flesh-colored cat suit strewn with Swarovski crystals from her video shoot.

Mike felt that odd feeling in the pit of his stomach again; the same feeling he'd had the night of their first date. He now recognized it as a warning…

The nominees in Destiny's category were announced shortly after she had performed her latest chart topper at the end of the show. She had only minutes to change from her performance outfit back into her evening gown; thank God the show had to break for commercials! There wasn't even time to get back to her seat in the audience and tightly clutch Mike's hand. She crossed her fingers and held her breath behind the curtains as one presenter tore open the envelope.

"And the winner is…Destiny Jordan!"

Her knees almost buckled. She had gone up against some heavy hitters, music industry's elite and the fans had chosen her. She forced herself not to scream, or cry, or make a complete fool of herself as she walked carefully onto the stage. It wasn't her first award. She had a few under her belt: Grammy's, People's Choice, VMA's, Billboard, World Music…but this was *the* American Music Award. This was 'Artist of The Year,' the most prestigious award in the entire show. Something she had coveted for years.

It had finally happened for her and it felt awesome!

***

Backstage in her dressing room, Destiny threw everyone except Mike out. A bottle of champagne was chilling in a silver bucket and a tray of matching flutes was on standby, but Destiny wasn't interested in drinking. She was already intoxicated with the thrill of scooping up the award for 'Artist of The Year' and performing live in front of an audience of millions. She was living her dream!

Mike's eyes locked with Destiny's as he removed the award from her trembling hands. It was a special moment and he didn't want anything getting in the way. He started kissing her and soon discovered that he didn't want to stop. She tasted like every delicious, forbidden thing he had ever imagined combined. His hands took on a life of their own—it seemed as though he couldn't stop touching her. Mike caught a glimpse of himself in the vanity table mirror…there was an eerie look in his eyes of a man who knew he had reached the point of no return.

Destiny gazed up at him with a dazed expression. The moment she had fantasized about for months had finally arrived and it was happening in a dressing room backstage at an awards show. "Wait…not here…not like this."

"You're right," he replied in a strained voice. "Let's get out of here. *Now*."

Mike stared numbly through an enormous rain-spattered window at the twinkling, slumbering city below. He leaned his forehead against the cool glass and closed his eyes, but could not escape the memory of what had occurred a short time ago.

They had barely made it through the front door of Destiny's hotel room.

Evidence in the form of articles of clothing and undergarments were strewn in a condemning trail which ended at the foot of the bed and there had been nothing tender or loving about what they had engaged in. He was disgusted by his lack of restraint.

Mike realized belatedly that he had been kidding himself all along. What made him think that he could stay true to God and His Word *and* have a ridiculously hot, unsaved girlfriend? Now all he could think about was how far he had fallen. He knew that resisting Destiny would be almost impossible now, because he had become one with her on an entirely different level. He vaguely wondered if she was on the Pill. It had never occurred to him to ask, since he hadn't planned on being intimate with her and neither of them had paused long enough to discuss using a condom. After all of those months of playing with fire they had finally ended up in bed having irresponsible, unsafe sex.

He looked over his shoulder at the beauty sleeping in the king-sized bed.

Was he sorry that it had happened?

No. However, he was sorry about *how* it had happened. Now they were just another fornicating tabloid couple.

As if on cue, Destiny woke up searching for him. "Mike?"

He should have made a clean getaway while she was sleeping; now they had to face each other and he was dreading it. He suddenly felt awkward with her and ashamed for not practicing what he'd been preaching. What was it about sin that felt so good, so *natural*, while one participated in it, but left one feeling so dirty afterwards?

Mike knew that it was the devil's plan to make him feel guilty and convicted after sin, but he couldn't seem to snap out of it. He felt as though he had let the entire tri-state area down.

"I'm over here," he said in the semidarkness.

"Why?" she asked, propping herself up on an elbow.

"I couldn't sleep."

Destiny patted the space on the bed beside her. "Wanna talk about it?" she asked softly, ignoring an unexpected twinge when he hesitated. He finally came and sat down on the edge of the bed and she could tell from his posture just how uncomfortable he was. "I know that you're sorry we—"

"It has nothing to do with you."

"How can you say that? It has *everything* to do with me!"

"But I *chose* to give in. I chose to sin and I knew better."

Destiny crossed her arms and blew a strand of hair out of her face. "So, what now? You're going to beat yourself up about it for the next 20 years?" She inhaled sharply as another thought occurred to her. "Are you going to leave me?"

"That would be hard…considering I'm in love with you,"

he softly replied. The thought of not seeing her again was too painful to contemplate.

Destiny kissed his shoulder. "Please don't beat yourself up because of what we did. You weren't alone in this bed and I have no regrets."

Mike gazed at her, wishing he could make her understand, but the more he looked at her swathed in soft blue Egyptian cotton sheets, the more he realized that the urge to be one with her was coming upon him again with a vengeance.

"I have to go," he said huskily.

"Don't. I want you to stay with me," she pleaded, taking him by the hand.

"If I stay we'll end up making love again," he said shaking his head.

Destiny had no idea how to respond. She had just experienced the most incredible, magical evening of her life and this man couldn't work past his religious woes long enough to spend the night with her. *What was wrong with this picture?*

She was stunned when he actually got up and started getting dressed.

"There's nowhere on Earth that I'd rather be than here with you, Destiny, but I can't stay," Mike admitted as he paused with one hand on the bedroom door. "No matter what happens after tonight, never forget how much I love you."

***

Back in his own hotel room, Mike turned the shower on. It seemed as though he couldn't get the water hot enough. He felt unclean and even after an hour of showering guilt and condemnation would not leave him. Images of everything he had just engaged in relentlessly bombarded him.

Tears combined with the shower water as he knelt helplessly down in the bathtub. "What have I done, Father? *What have I done?*"

Chapter 13

Destiny stared at the article. The caption said, "Paradise Lost?" and had a photo of her and Mike looking miserable and distant as they shared a stretch limo to LAX. The inside story was loaded with colorful details about a romantic tryst gone horribly wrong. According to the hotel staff, Mike hadn't even spent the night with his lady love after doing the dirty deed. The accuracy of it killed her.

The press never gave her a break. It was moments like this that Destiny hated them.

"I feel for the brother," Chelsea said, looking over her shoulder.

"Thanks for your support," Destiny muttered, as she flung the paper into the trash.

"You're welcome. I do have to give him some credit, though—that's the longest I've ever seen any man resist you!" Chelsea said with a bittersweet smile. She could only imagine how tormented the cop had to be feeling. "So, how's he holding up?"

"I'm not sure," Destiny said solemnly. "I haven't heard from him in days. You think I should call?"

Chelsea just shook her head. If that had been *her* man, calling him would have been the last thing on her mind. She would have been at his apartment, banging the door down and begging him to forgive her. "I think you should give him some space and let him work a few things out. It can't be easy being a church youth leader one day and then burning up the sheets with the AMA's *Artist of the Year* the next."

Destiny sighed heavily. "This relationship has been a struggle for him. I wish I'd met him before he hooked up with Jesus!"

"Just be grateful you met him at all and try to be more supportive about the total package and not just the parts that interest you the most!" Chelsea said in Mike's defense.

"Wow—somebody woke up on the wrong side of the bed

this morning," Destiny said, wondering if she shouldn't be a little offended by her assistant's comment.

"*Somebody* isn't letting your behind off the hook," Chelsea countered, wagging a finger in Destiny's direction. "Stop being so selfish and thinking only about what *you* want and not what he wants or needs."

Destiny opened her mouth with a quick rebuttal, but Chelsea shut her down with a look.

"If you knew that it would be another six months before you had sex with Mike again would you stick around? Please feel free to be honest."

Destiny folded her arms tightly. Chelsea was like an older sister to her, but sometimes she crossed the line with her opinions about Destiny's personal life. Still, there were times that it forced Destiny to take a hard look at herself and analyze her actions. She knew that Chelsea was fond of Mike and didn't want to see him get hurt, but Destiny also knew that her assistant was very disappointed in her for sleeping with him.

"You're taking this way too personally. Why are you really upset with me?" Destiny finally asked.

"Because you had a good thing going with Mike and its five minutes away from going up in smoke because you can't control your libido and could care less that he's a good man trying to live right!"

"Chelsea, why are you speaking as if things are already over?"

"Because I know how quickly you lose interest after you've been intimate with a man."

Destiny inhaled sharply. "I can't believe you just said that."

"It's true, Destiny. I'm not trying to hurt or upset you. These past six years I've been your personal assistant, your stylist and your therapist. I've seen and heard it all. Mike is the best thing that ever happened to you and all you could focus on all of these months is how to get him between the sheets. It's time to grow up, or you're going to lose him."

"He wanted to have sex, too, you know," Destiny said

defensively.

"Did he really? Or was he just worn out from your tempting and pursuing him?"

"I know what I felt…it wasn't my imagination. Mike wanted to be with me. He puts his heart and soul into *everything* he does."

"I'm sure he does," Chelsea said sarcastically, as she watched Destiny march indignantly out of the room. The only part of Mike that probably didn't enjoy the sin was his spirit and if he had been listening it would have told him to get out of Dodge before it was too late.

Chapter 14

It was New Year's Day and Destiny was feeling miserable and not because she'd overindulged at some party while the countdown was taking place in Times Square. The holidays were usually her favorite time of the year; she would have a blast putting up a tree, decorating her condo, lighting seasonal candles, playing holiday CD's and attending parties. Every now and then she even hopped a plane to London to celebrate the holidays with her parents. But this year was different. She could care less about ornaments and turkey sides. She hadn't heard from Mike since the awards show fiasco and despite what he had said that final night, she was certain he had dumped her and moved on. Plus, she was sure that she had the Flu.

When she began throwing up at the mere thought of food and skipped a period, she realized that it wasn't simply depression or a virus ailing her. Fortunately, she had a pregnancy kit leftover from a false alarm she'd had with a prior lover and the expiration date was still good...

Destiny tried to relax while she waited for the test results, but it was next to impossible. She jumped up from the edge of the toilet seat and began pacing the enormous master bathroom of her condo.

She couldn't be pregnant! She just couldn't.

And she didn't want to be either. Call her selfish, but her career was the moment's priority. She wasn't even remotely interested in being someone's mother.

If she were a smoker she'd have blown through an entire pack to steady her nerves by now. Why—in this age of modern technology—a woman had to wait at all for a pregnancy test result was beyond her.

She gulped down a second glass of wine and then glanced at the clock on her bedroom wall. It was time.

She could see the two pink lines before she even picked up the test stick. And they weren't just pink, they were *dark* pink, almost as though the test was daring her to deny their existence. It had to be wrong. The kit supplied two additional tests. She'd just try another one.

But even as she tore into the packaging of the second test she had a sinking feeling in the pit of her stomach.

"It's one o'clock in the morning, Destiny. This had better be good," a groggy Chelsea said as she fumbled for the switch on her lamp.

"I'm pregnant."

"*What*?! Wait—are you okay?" Destiny sounded like someone had died on the other end of the line she was crying so hard.

"What am I going to do, Chelsea? I can't do this!"

"The first thing you're going to do is calm down. You're not the first female in history to experience an unplanned pregnancy," Chelsea said sensibly, wanting to slap the taste out of Destiny's mouth for having unprotected sex in the first place. "The second thing you're going to do is call Mike."

"I don't know…"

"He's got a right to make some decisions, too. You didn't make that baby by yourself."

"I know, I just feel so trapped right now."

"He's a good man, Destiny and the best thing that ever happened to your sorry behind, in my humble opinion."

"I can't believe you just said that," Destiny sniffled.

"You'll get over it. Now go and call him. You'll feel a whole lot better after you let him know what's going on."

"I hope so. Considering I haven't heard from him since the awards show."

Chelsea chuckled softly. "Girl, I'm willing to bet this news will get his *immediate* attention!"

For some reason, that comment didn't make Destiny feel any better. "Thanks, Chelsea," she said softly.

"Hey, it's not just my job, it's an adventure!" her assistant said dryly. "Everything's going to be fine. Just let me know how it goes—preferably some time after lunch!"

64

"I will, and sorry for waking you."

***

"Hey," Destiny said softly, when Mike finally picked up the phone.

"Hey," he replied unenthusiastically.

"We need to talk."

"I know. I'm sorry for my behavior these past few weeks."

"That's not why I called you...the reason I called is... well...because...I'm pregnant." There was a very long pause and Destiny wondered if he was still there. She forced herself to not chew nervously on a thumbnail.

"But we were only intimate one time," he finally reasoned.

"Technically it was one *night*, not one *time*. Are you angry?" she asked momentarily holding her breath.

"No, of course not. I'm just shocked."

"This doesn't have to be a problem for us, you know."

"What do you mean?"

"I don't have to have this baby. I mean, we didn't plan it and—"

"Absolutely not!" he said firmly.

"Why?"

"Destiny, before I got saved I was a Catholic for many years. I'm pro-life, so if you wanted to get rid of our baby you shouldn't have mentioned it to me."

"Mike, *I don't want it.*"

"You're just scared...parenthood is a big step."

"No, I'm not ready to be someone's mother!"

"But you were ready to hop in bed with *someone's* father?"

"Oh, don't judge me! I didn't put a gun to your head that night! Neither of us planned this pregnancy, so why go through with it?!"

"I'll tell you what—you have an abortion and we're finished!" he said, slamming the phone down in her ear.

Destiny stared at her cordless.

That was not the Mike Reilly she knew and had fallen in love with.

At four in the morning, building security called to let Destiny know that Mike was downstairs. She told them to go ahead and allow him to come up.

Mike was leaning against the doorframe of her condo by the time she finally pulled herself together. Wordlessly, she stepped aside and he headed towards the kitchen, a remorseful look on his handsome face.

"I know it's late, but I couldn't sleep," he lamely explained.

"It's okay. I couldn't sleep either," she admitted. "You want some tea?"

"Sure, as long as it's got some caffeine in it."

They went into the kitchen and Destiny put a sunny antique kettle on the stove. She turned to face him and noticed that he was looking at her strangely. "You're not going to get all weird on me now, are you?"

"I can't help it. I haven't stopped thinking about it since the moment you told me."

"Well don't start passing out cigars just yet, Officer Reilly. I'm still not sure about all this."

"You think I am?" he asked. "Until recently, we were a couple and now—"

"Exactly. Now we're *what*?"

"We're whatever you want us to be, Destiny. The ball's in your court. All I ask is that you don't kill our baby."

Her eyes were suddenly brimming with tears. "I'd already thought I had lost you and now *this*! What's going to happen to us?"

"What's going to happen to your career?" he countered knowingly.

"That, too! The media is merciless if you gain a few pounds and don't shed the weight a few weeks after delivering," she complained.

Mike sheltered her in his arms. "Don't worry, I'm not going anywhere. I just needed a little space. I'm sorry I hurt you."

"I forgive you," she said with a sigh. "I love you so much."

"Enough to marry me?" he asked, taking the plunge with

or without God's consent.

Destiny almost stopped breathing. The last time they had discussed marriage he had insisted that his wife had to be saved, and they both knew that nothing had changed for her spiritually. Was he making an exception because of her condition?

"I can't tell whether that was a yes or no," Mike teased, transfixing her with those gorgeous aqua eyes.

"You're serious," she breathed, still reeling from his impromptu proposal.

"You noticed," he said.

"Yes," she said with a dazed expression. "I'll marry you."

"You're not going to change your mind in the morning?" he asked.

"It's already morning," she absently replied, momentarily thinking of how the media was going to have a ball with this latest news. Her life was about to become a bigger circus than it already was and part of her wondered if she was up for it. In the meantime, since technically they were now engaged…

"So, you interested in spending the night?" she asked slyly.

Mike nearly groaned. Destiny had no idea about the spiritual and emotional rollercoaster ride he'd been on the past few weeks. There was no way he was going near her again without the comfort of a wedding band.

"It's not like you could get me pregnant," she teased.

"I think I'll wait," he replied, trying not to chuckle.

"You make me want to scream!" she said blowing air through clenched teeth.

"Be patient and try to get some rest. I'll stop by later this evening."

"Don't go," she murmured, wrapping her arms around his waist. "It's not every day a girl gets proposed to."

"I have to, honey. Dream about me," he said, kissing her lightly on the mouth.

"Always," she vowed, gazing up at him.

Chapter 15

"You look like you've got a lot on your mind, Reilly. What's eatin' you?"

"Destiny's pregnant," Mike said as a matter of fact.

"No way!" Ramirez exclaimed before he could catch himself. As far as he knew, thanks to the internet and every other type of media, Reilly had only touched the singer one time. Then another thought crossed his mind. "It's yours, right?"

Mike gave his partner a withering look and Ramirez threw his hands up in self defense. "Man, I knew that abstinence thing wouldn't last forever."

"What's that supposed to mean?"

"C'mon, Reilly! I know you're a Christian, but you're still a man, and you're dating a woman who was just on the cover of *Maxim* for crying out loud!"

"I'm going to marry her, Ramirez," Mike said solemnly, as he shoved a foot into his Nike cross-trainer.

"*What*?! Hey, you know I usually stay out of your business—" Ramirez began carefully.

"So, you're turning over a new leaf? What's on your mind, Ramirez?"

"You had a slip-up, but don't marry her," his partner replied.

"I'm going to pretend that I didn't hear you say that."

"Mike, is that really the kind of life you want? Not even able to go to the supermarket without somebody taping your every move? Having to be her personal bodyguard every time she walks out the door? Besides, she's never around! You're going to be raising that kid by yourself! You deserve better than that. I just want you to think about what you're getting yourself into."

"I have thought about it," Mike said with finality.

"Would you have thought about it if she hadn't gotten pregnant?"

"Boy, you're not pulling any punches today, are you, Ramirez?"

"I care about you, man! We've been partners forever. I just don't want to see you get hurt. I know that you're old fashioned and trying to do the right thing, but sometimes doing the right thing can be the wrong thing. Trust me, I know what I'm talking about."

Mike slammed his locker shut and stared at his partner for a moment. "You don't understand."

"Sure I do. Destiny's beyond hot, rich, talented and pregnant with *your* kid. After the shock wears off you'll probably have moments when you feel like you've just won the Lottery! Just be sure you know what you're getting yourself into."

"I am sure. That's my baby she's carrying, not a 'slip-up' and we're going to be a family."

Ramirez was silent for a moment. "I'll always have your back, Reilly, but this is one time I don't agree with you. Hopefully I won't ever have to say 'I told you so.' "

Chapter 16

"I know that I didn't do this the right way the first time around, so—" Mike said with a dimpled grin, as he knelt down in front of Destiny two weeks later and presented her with a small, aqua-colored velvet box wrapped with a delicate silver ribbon.

Destiny was touched, as always, by the heart of Mike Reilly and immediately grew tearful as she accepted the gift. Her hands trembled noticeably when she lifted the lid and gasped aloud.

Nestled inside the velvet box was a flawless, round, three-carat diamond ring flanked on either side by one-carat aquamarine gemstones in a stunning platinum vintage setting. Destiny had an idea about how much the piece must have cost him and knew that unless he had some money saved up, he'd probably be paying that ring off for the next ten years. It only made it that much more precious to her.

"Mike," she choked, her voice thick with emotion. "You didn't have to do this."

"I wanted to."

"It's exquisite—I love the aquamarines," she murmured.

"They're so you'll never forget me," he replied softly, as he slid the ring onto her finger and kissed her tenderly.

Destiny wrapped her arms around his neck and hugged him. "Thank you...it's the most beautiful gift anyone's ever given to me!"

"The feeling's mutual," he replied, gazing at her intently.

She blushed uncharacteristically and lowered her lashes.

What was it about this man that left her speechless?

"Now that we're official, you ready to meet my family?" he asked with a boyish grin.

Destiny's eyes widened. Now she really was speechless.

***

"You're just going to meet the man's family," Chelsea said as she brushed past her boss.

"Stop reminding me!" Destiny exclaimed, falling

backwards on her bed. "What am I going to wear?!" she wailed.

"That's what this is really all about, isn't it?"

"First impressions *are* everything—"

Chelsea figured that if any of Mike's family members had ever seen any of her music videos it was too late for first impressions. But she wisely kept her thoughts to herself.

"Destiny, this is a good thing, this is *normal*," Chelsea said encouragingly. "These people are going to be your baby's relatives."

"What if they don't like me?" she asked, her eyes widening with the awful possibility.

Chelsea forced herself not to roll her own eyes. "They're going to love you! Just relax and be your cute, funny lil' self—pretend you're on a talk show when they start asking questions!" Chelsea handed Destiny a pair of $300 jeans (instead of the usual $700 pair) and a caramel-colored top that didn't scream video vixen. She paired the outfit with coordinating booties and basic gold accessories. "Now, get dressed."

Destiny gave Chelsea a grateful smile. "What would I do without you?"

"Hopefully you'll never have to find out!"

"One of *People* magazine's *50 Most Beautiful*! Talk about aiming high," Mike's sister said as she reached into the fridge for dessert. She was not happy about her brother's relationship with this particular celebrity and she wasn't going to be shy with her opinions. Her friends and coworkers were in awe, but she personally wanted better for Mike.

"What's that supposed to mean?" he asked, placing a kettle of water on the stove.

"We don't want you to get hurt is what your sister means," his mother said, entering the kitchen carrying an empty casserole dish.

"Where's Destiny?" he asked his mother.

"In the den with your father and brother—who, by the way, is more in love with her than you are."

"If you don't like her feel free to say it…but, I'm still

going to marry her."

"Michael, she's charming, funny and beautiful—what's not to like?" his mom asked, looking up at her son with patient eyes. "But I'm afraid for you."

"Don't be, Ma. Everything's gonna be okay. You'll see."

"Always the optimist!" his sister said, rolling her eyes. "Ma, you should see the kind of videos that girl makes—she sets women back 400 years!"

"Shush! Remember that she's a guest in our home," their mother chastised.

"A *guest* my brother is going to marry!"

"Accept it, sis. I love her, she loves me and well, she did say yes."

"What does your pastor have to say about all of this?" his sister pressed.

"You never know when to draw the line do you?" Mike asked, finally irritated.

"I'm just curious."

"You're just nosey!"

"Stop it, both of you! Michael, what *did* your pastor have to say?"

Mike exhaled slowly. They were going to find out the truth sooner or later. Better from him than a tabloid. "My pastor said that I can be a great father to our baby without becoming Destiny's husband."

His mother eased silently down into a chair, shaking her head. "Oh, Michael," was all she could say.

His sister cussed and stormed out of the kitchen.

The tea kettle whistled and Mike turned the burner off. He looked pointedly at his mother. "Shall we tell dad before or after dessert?"

"I take it your family wasn't thrilled by our news," Destiny said soberly, as Mike parked in front of her building.

He studiously avoided eye contact with her.

"Your sister mysteriously vanished after dinner, your mom suddenly had a headache and your dad looked like he'd

72

aged twenty years! If your brother hadn't given me a hug at the end of the night—"

"What do you want me to say, Destiny?" he asked, finally looking at her. "They're disappointed about our baby being conceived outside of marriage, they're nervous about their son being engaged to a celebrity…it's a lot to absorb…try to see things from their perspective."

"No! I may be many things, but I'm still a human being with feelings and whether they like it or not, it's still *their* grandbaby growing inside of me!"

"Honey—"

"Don't you *honey* me! Just remember: this was *your* bright idea! This isn't the movies—I didn't have to meet the parents! We're both over 30!"

Mike didn't attempt to stop Destiny as she slammed his car door shut and stormed off. A security guard was already waiting outside her building to escort her inside, so he knew she would be safe. He leaned his head back against the leather headrest and sighed.

Chapter 17

Destiny wanted to get married before her baby bump grew too large, so time was of the essence. She had quickly gotten over the disappointing dinner with Mike's family and was thumbing through bridal magazines again. Lately, it was the high point of her day. She groaned when the telephone rang, because she had three more to look through and didn't want any distractions. "Chelsea!"

"I already have it! It's Bill and he said that if you don't pick up and speak with him immediately, he'll take the subway over here, so help him—"

This was serious. Bill *never* took mass transportation. Destiny giggled and picked up the cordless from her nightstand. Chelsea came into her room to watch the fireworks.

"Hi, Bill," she said sweetly.

"Oh, so it takes my making threats to brave the rat-infested subway system of this once-great city to get you on a phone?" he huffed.

"Don't be so melodramatic—"

"Look, I've got every supermarket rag in and out of town breathing down my neck and I need some answers, pronto! So are you going to help me do my job or do I start fabricating?"

Destiny grimaced. Chelsea grinned.

"Fine! You want to give me the silent treatment? Then this is what we're going to do: ridiculously huge—bigger than Mariah's *first* wedding huge! I'm thinking 500 guests *minimum*—"

"Bill, I already told you—*no big wedding*! I don't care about what the media would love! They'll turn it into a circus and the city will be tied up with gridlocks! It's our special day and we're going to do it our way!" she rolled her eyes at Chelsea. "Now, I'm in the middle of something super important. Give me a couple of hours—I promise I'll call you back." She promptly hung up before the griping began.

"Wait, don't tell me. He wants it held at a Park Avenue cathedral with media coverage from here to Fashion Avenue, right?"

"Worse. He wants to fill the cathedral with 500 warm bodies," Destiny said with a frown. "It's not Bill's fault—he is the best PR rep in the city. I can handle the over-the-top celebrity wedding scene, but Mike can't. Friends and family are one thing, but the excess media attention and fans…"

"Girl, you know it goes with the territory," Chelsea said stifling a yawn. "And he should know it too, by now."

"Yeah, well…"

"Why don't the two of you just elope?"

"And disappoint my fans?" Destiny looked aghast.

"You can still wear a fabulous dress at a civil ceremony," Chelsea teased, knowing her boss wouldn't be caught dead in some local courthouse in her designer wedding gown.

"I don't think so!"

"Who would you like to invite?"

"Do I look like I know 500 people?"

"Okayyy, we'll revisit that one at a later date. Are you in the mood to look at cake designs and invites?"

Destiny looked tired and bored. She wanted to get back to her magazines so she'd have some idea about what she was going to wear.

"I'm going to call one of those celebrity wedding planners," Chelsea decided.

"Alright, but please make sure that everything gets approved by you—"

"You know I will."

Destiny grinned. "You couldn't keep your hands off this one if you tried!"

"Don't flatter yourself," Chelsea said with a sniff. "Where are you off to?"

"The bathroom."

"Again?"

"Hey, it goes with the territory!"

***

As the weeks wore on, Chelsea soon discovered that the only thing that Destiny *was* excited about was her wedding gown and with her changing waist line, her dress had to be comfortable, yet trendy and possibly empire cut, sans a train. A Parisian designer was finally commissioned for the job and he handled everything from Destiny's tiara and veil to the coordinating matte peep-toe pumps embroidered with Swarovski crystals. And in the end, despite the wedding planner's best efforts to handle everything for the Jordan-Reilly wedding, Chelsea did what she did best and intervened in everything from the flower arrangements to the cake design. After all, who knew her boss better than she did?

Destiny became Mrs. Reilly on a chilly day in March. Mike's partner, Ramirez, showed up for the ceremony, even though he had declined the offer of best man. In his heart, he still felt as though his friend was making a serious mistake. Fortunately, Mike's brother was a shoo-in for the job. He didn't share his family's sentiments about his future sister-in-law. He just thought his brother was the luckiest guy on the planet. One of Destiny's closest girlfriends—a notorious choreographer—was the maid of honor. (Chelsea made a mental note to keep an eye on *that* one and Mike's younger brother. It was obvious that he was easily star struck and she wanted the young man to leave the ceremony with his innocence intact.) Surprisingly, Mike's parents came to the wedding, though his mother barely smiled. His sister was a no show. Destiny's parents flew in from England, so that her father could walk her down the aisle and her mother could have her 15 minutes of fame with the American press.

Security from her condo to the undisclosed wedding site was extremely tight, because someone had already notified the press about the wedding date and paparazzi had camped out nearby in the hopes of getting some 'money shots.' When Destiny emerged from her lobby she was carefully, but rapidly ushered into a white Rolls Royce stretch with tinted glass. Everything was so organized and handled so professionally that no one was able to even get close enough without getting cut off by officers from Mike's precinct; his brothers in blue were there to ensure that order was maintained. Fans that had gathered only caught a glimpse of Destiny as she was whisked away and members of the media had to settle for taking their photos from a distance.

In an additional effort to deter fans and paparazzi from ruining the event, Bill had a friend in the industry spread a rumor that Destiny and her new husband would be flying out from JFK to some tropical locale. In truth, the limo driver, Sam, would be taking the newlyweds to a location that was close to home, quiet and very secluded. The couple would be spending their week-long honeymoon at a Victorian mansion in New Paltz, where an entire floor of a mansion had been secured for their privacy...

Chapter 18

The honeymoon suite was exquisite. The décor looked like something from a bygone era. There were crystal vases of calla lilies and the king-sized, four-poster bed was strewn with fragrant ivory and blush-colored rose petals. The fireplace glowed invitingly and a bottle of champagne and Tiffany glasses beckoned to them from a cherry wood nightstand.

Destiny laughed with delight as Mike carried her over the threshold and deposited her in the center of the bed. She had never been happier.

"Bone of my bones, flesh of my flesh…," Mike murmured, as he gazed lovingly into her eyes.

Destiny smiled affectionately at him. This man was too deep for her sometimes. "Who said that and what book is it in?"

"Adam to Eve, Genesis 2:23," he replied, nuzzling her neck.

"Wonder what inspired him to say that," she breathed.

"We'll analyze it later…"

"Okay," she said slowly, "but I've got to tell you…"

"Yes, Mrs. Reilly?"

"We're starved!" she declared, patting her gently rounded belly.

Mike handed her a menu. Fifteen minutes later he was calling room service. "Good evening. Thank you, yes, everything's perfect. We'd like to start with the Artisan cheese plate and the Maryland blue crab cakes and for the entrees, the pan-seared chicken breast with bread pudding and rosemary cream and grilled NY strip steak with shallot mashed potatoes and chasseur sauce. For dessert? The Chocolate Explosion and the caramel mascarpone apple cake with pomegranate sauce. Could we also have a pitcher of sweetened iced tea and coffee with that? Thanks."

Destiny clapped her hands with childish delight. "Yummy! Can't wait—it all sounds delicious!"

"The appetizers will be up in a little while—"

"Great! Just enough time for a quick shower!" she said with a wink, as she darted off the bed and into the spacious bathroom.

Mike reached for the television's remote.

Destiny stuck her head outside the bathroom door. "Hey, you gonna join me or what?"

"I didn't know I was invited," Mike replied with mock indifference.

She rolled her eyes and then crooked a finger. "It's our wedding night! Will you please stop being a gentleman for at least 24 hours? Get your fine self over here on the double, Officer Reilly!"

Grinning, her husband did exactly as he was told.

The following morning, Destiny sat contemplatively watching the sun rise behind the snow-capped mountains from her tower room. She paused momentarily and gazed at the handsome cop sleeping beneath the rumpled covers and sighed. Last night had been exceptional. Everything about Mike Reilly was so incredible…so perfect.

It terrified her.

Every romantic relationship prior to this one had been a counterfeit. Mike Reilly loved completely, with his spirit, soul and body. She had never met anyone like him.

Destiny wanted to be the perfect wife for him and the perfect mother for their child, but inwardly she questioned her ability to follow through. When she agreed to marry Mike she had given her consent based on her emotional state at the moment and now she questioned the wisdom of her decision.

Her life had always been about her. From the very first, her parents had realized that they'd been blessed with a beautiful as well as talented child and although Destiny did not seriously pursue singing until she was a teen, there was never a doubt in anyone's mind that she was destined for greatness. It had come so easily for her and so quickly; almost as though it had simply been waiting for her to mature before it introduced itself to her.

Now she wondered how being married and having a baby

were going to affect her popularity. Would the public forget about her? Would her male fans get turned off by the wedding band? Would she get fat and not be able to shed the baby weight after the delivery?

Destiny had worked herself up into a near mental frenzy when she was startled by a strong hand with a platinum and diamond band caressing her shoulder.

Her guardian angel was awake.

"Good morning, Mrs. Reilly," Mike said, kissing the back of her bared neck.

"Mike!" Destiny exclaimed, jumping up from the beautifully upholstered chair and wrapping her arms tightly around his waist. "I love you so much!"

"I love you, too—" he replied, a bit bewildered.

"I want to make you the happiest man in the world!"

"Okay…"

"Let's go back to bed," she said, looking up at him with luminous eyes.

"Woman after my own heart," he laughed, scooping her up in his arms.

***

It was evening and their fourth day as newlyweds; Destiny was ready to leave their suite and do some exploring. She was surprised to discover the array of recreations and amenities available to guests. Earlier in the day they had enjoyed a tour of the mansion and a visit to the spa. She'd been sweet to the staff and signed a few autographs and even introduced herself to the head chef in order to personally thank him for his superb cuisine. Tomorrow, she and Mike planned to go ice skating, or perhaps on a sleigh ride. She could hardly wait!

Snow had fallen late that afternoon, blanketing the mountains and surrounding countryside with a shimmering white coat and the sky had changed from stormy gray to a deep clear indigo sprinkled with stars. It was serene, enchanting, and idyllic. Destiny made a mental note to give Chelsea a raise as soon as she returned home.

"Come here, I want to share something with you," Mike

80

coaxed with a dimpled smile and outstretched hand.

She sighed and slipped her hand into his. This phenomenal man was her husband now. No more running away, no more game playing. This was for keeps. This was forever.

He patted an overstuffed sofa and she sat down attentively, admiring his chiseled profile and the shape of his hands as he lifted a navy leather-bound book.

"Shapely and graceful your sandaled feet, and queenly your movement—your limbs are lithe and elegant, the work of a master artist. Your body is a chalice, wine-filled. Your skin is silken and tawny like a field of wheat touched by the breeze. Your breasts are like fawns, twins of a gazelle. Your neck is carved ivory, curved and slender. Your eyes are wells of light, deep with mystery. Quintessentially feminine! Your profile turns all heads, commanding attention. The feelings I get when I see the high mountain ranges —stirrings of desire, longings for the heights— remind me of you, and I'm spoiled for anyone else! Your beauty, within and without, is absolute, dear lover, close companion…"

Destiny was mesmerized. The man also read poetry? *Was he for real?* She didn't know whether it was the verse he was reading, or the way the flames in the fireplace were reflected in his aquamarine eyes, but she felt herself falling for Officer Reilly all over again. He had put the book down and was gazing at her expectantly, but Destiny was captivated, the drink in her hand untouched. Mike playfully waved his hands in front of her face until he got her attention.

"What was that?" she breathed.

"The Bible. Song of Solomon, Chapter 7. Not exactly the King James Version, but it works for me."

"I didn't know there was stuff like that in the Bible."

"Take a peek sometime, you'd be amazed," he suggested, removing the glass of iced tea from her hand before she broke the stem.

"*You're* amazing," she said, still basking. "That was seriously romantic."

"Thank you," Mike replied, pleased that she had liked it.

Destiny snuggled up beside him. She loved everything

about him. The way he looked, the way he smiled, the way he smelled. But most of all, she loved the way that he loved her and the little things he did to make her happy. There was so much in her heart, so much she wanted to say to him and she hoped that he could see it all in her eyes.

"*Beloved,*" he whispered as their lips brushed.

"Song of Solomon?" she asked softly.

He nodded meaningfully, as they embraced and their hearts momentarily beat as one.

Chapter 19

When Destiny and Mike returned from their honeymoon, the first thing Mike decided to do was go to church and see if Pastor Hammond was available. He wanted to let his pastor know that everything had worked out fine after all. Actually, he also wanted to find out why his pastor had not come to his wedding.

But, upon entering the lobby, Mike was surprised to run into one of the teens from his youth group. She looked distraught and as though she'd been crying.

"Hi, Brother Mike," she mumbled, swiping at her nose with the sleeve of her hoodie.

"Hi, Karen, what are you doing here?"

"I'm supposed to meet with Deacon Sheila."

"Have you been waiting long?"

"Um, a little. She called on her cell; she's running late because of traffic."   "What's wrong?" Mike asked softly with a concerned expression.

The teen momentarily looked as though she wasn't going to respond; she jumped up from the bench she'd been perched on and began pacing frantically. Suddenly, she whirled around to face Mike, an anguished expression in her eyes. "It's all over the news—on the Internet, in the papers—how could you run off and marry *her*?! I mean, it was nice of her to come and hang out that Friday night and sing for us, but she doesn't even look like she's *thinking* about Jesus!"

Mike sighed heavily. He had no idea what to say to the disgruntled teen.

"You're the one who taught us that two can't stand if they're not in agreement. You said to pray and to wait on God and when the season was right that God had the perfect mate for everyone! Did you get tired of waiting, Brother Mike? Because I can't see how a woman with a gazillion websites that guys drool over every day could possibly be the perfect mate for our favorite youth leader!"

Mike was stumped. How could he help Karen to understand

that too often God's plans and man's plans didn't coincide?

"Just help me to understand, Brother Mike," the teen said brokenly. "Because if *you* can be out of God's will then there's no hope for the rest of us!"

"First of all, you've got to get me off that imaginary pedestal, Karen. Even the Bible says that all of our 'righteousness are as filthy rags.' There's only one who was and is perfect—and His name isn't Mike Reilly."

"So are the rumors true, then? Is Destiny pregnant with your baby? Is that why you married her?"

Mike paused momentarily, questioning the wisdom of sharing such personal information. In the end, he decided that since honesty and truth was what he had always tried to instill in the church's youth he wasn't going to stop now.

"Yes, Karen. Destiny's pregnant with my baby."

The girl inhaled sharply. Shock and disappointment were written all over her young face.

Mike gave her a moment to compose herself.

"H-how do you feel about it?" she finally continued in a small voice. "I mean, since she's not saved."

"Honestly? A little uncertain sometimes; but, sometimes I'm just excited about being a new husband and dad."

"But more about being a new dad? Right?"

"What do you mean, Karen?"

"Well, Destiny could always decide that she's more interested in the limelight than being married and you could possibly give up on having an unsaved wife one day, but a baby is forever, right?"

Mike was confused about the teen's logic. *Where was she going with all of this?*
It was suddenly vitally important to understand what was going on inside her head. "A baby's a huge responsibility, Karen, married or not. Is there something you'd—"

"I'm pregnant!" she blurted and then immediately burst into tears.

Mike felt like kicking himself; he felt partially responsible. If he hadn't spent so much time pursuing Destiny and shirking

84

his responsibilities with the youth group this might not have happened. Karen had been a troubled teen who had to be handled with kid gloves from the very beginning and Mike had heard rumors about an older boyfriend who was constantly sniffing around her doorstep. Apparently the young man had finally gotten what he'd been looking for.

"Karen, are you sure?"

"I bought three of those home pregnancy kits *and* went to Planned Parenthood last week. I'm three months."

Mike rubbed both eyes with the heel of one of his hands. He would have to inform his pastor and the girl's parents. Not something he was thrilled about doing since he wasn't serving in the ministry at the current time and should not even be having this conversation with one of their youth.

"Karen, why didn't you use protection?" he asked as carefully as he could.

"We did," she sniffled, her eyes and nose pink from sobbing. "It broke. Why didn't *you* use protection, Brother Mike?"

This kid had him feeling like an idiot. Mike wanted to shrug his shoulders and ignore the question the way an adolescent would, but truth had its way again.

"I was being irresponsible, Karen. Things got out of hand and it's like my flesh took over and I forgot who I was."

She slowly nodded her head with understanding. "It's funny how one romantic moment can turn into a nightmare so fast."

"Where's the baby's father?" Mike asked.

Karen snorted. "In the wind. He's 19 years old and getting ready to attend an Ivy League school in another state. The last thing he's thinking about is parenthood."

Her boyfriend should have been thinking about how he was going to stay out of jail for messing with a minor. Karen was only 16 and the Statutory Rape Law was still in effect the last time Mike had checked.

For now there were bigger fish to fry, though.

"What're you going to do?"

"What else can I do? I don't believe in abortion and it's not the baby's fault its here. I'm going to have it and give it up for adoption…and pray that my foster mom doesn't kick me to the curb for getting myself in this jam in the first place."

"I'm sorry that I haven't been here for you, Karen," Mike said sincerely.

The teen shrugged delicately. "You've got your own life and problems, Brother Mike and I'm a big girl. I knew what I was doing. I just didn't think I'd get caught."

Her words reverberated deep within his soul.

Hadn't he felt the same way while he was lying with Destiny? Like God was on hiatus and wouldn't find out about what they'd done until later?

How foolish he had been. How deceived. Satan had to be somewhere laughing his pitchfork off.

Play now and pay later.

That was the moral to both their stories. Only, both stories were still being written and Mike had no idea how either was going to turn out.

Chapter 20

"I don't like that video," Mike said one Saturday night. He and Destiny were lying down, eating tiramisu gelato and watching BET.

Destiny rolled her eyes. "What's wrong with it?"

"It's too racy, too suggestive."

"It's about *you*!" she replied, feeling her feathers starting to ruffle.

"I know, but that doesn't make it okay." His wife rolling around on a bed, playing with handcuffs and a nightstick, while she fantasized about some other guy in a uniform was not flattering to him at all. Even the tempo of the music sounded perverse to him.

"I'll change the channel," she said with a resigned expression.

Mike took the remote out of her hand. "You're my wife now and you're carrying our child. Try to remember that when your record label decides you need visuals to go with your music."

Furious, Destiny got out of bed and left the room.

She wanted to pour herself a glass of wine, but remembered her condition. Besides, she didn't want Saint Michael berating her. Lately, it seemed as though everything about her lifestyle got under his skin. She'd thought that marriage with Mike was a dream come true, but the truth was he got on her nerves. Between his badgering her to go to church, griping about her videos, commenting on how she spent her money, whining about how busy she always was…sometimes she wished they had just gone their separate ways after the awards show. She felt guilty for thinking it, but that was how she felt.

And she hated being pregnant. Hated the way her breasts fluffed up like water balloons and how the shape of her butt changed. Hated the fact that she couldn't safely streak her hair until after the first trimester and how her feet swelled until her Manolo's were too tight. Hated the exhaustion and constipation and lived in mortal fear of hemorrhoids and stretch marks.

She didn't want to be interviewed by any magazines, or talk show hosts, or even go outside for some fresh air. She didn't want *anyone* to see her this way. The glossy hair, gorgeous fingernails, and luminous skin which she had read about in the pregnancy books had obviously happened to someone else, because she didn't see any of those things when she looked in the mirror. Destiny could hardly wait for the whole thing to be over with, especially after the needle on her bathroom scale hit 180.

Finally, one hot summer evening she got her wish.

She was having another one of her crying fits when Chelsea arrived at the condo. A sarcastic comment was lurking on the tip of the personal assistant's tongue, but she decided to keep her mouth closed. She felt sorry for Mike, because living with Destiny these days had to feel like a prison sentence. She complained about everything and Chelsea was eternally grateful that the woman hadn't been challenged with morning sickness for too long because that would have just been one more thing for her to gripe about!

"Why don't you come over here and sit down? I'll get you a glass of juice," Chelsea said patiently.

"If it's not a mimosa I'm not interested!" Destiny groused, plopping down on her sofa.

"It's almost over, Destiny—"

"Almost over?! This brat is a week overdue and these friggin' Braxton Hicks contractions are killing me! How much longer am I supposed to—" Destiny suddenly gasped.

"What is it?" Chelsea asked, refraining from saying the word *now*.

"I think that's going to leave a stain," Destiny whispered, sliding away from the big wet spot beneath her bottom.

"Congratulations, girlfriend!" Chelsea said cheerfully. "Your water just broke!"

***

"Am I wearing a cape with an 'S' on the back?" Destiny hissed, grabbing the nurse's arm.

"N–no," the young woman sputtered, almost dropping a

pitcher of ice chips.

"Then would you please get the anesthesiologist in here before I commit a homicide?!" she screeched as another contraction hit her.

Chelsea smiled apologetically at the nurse and pried Destiny's fingers loose. "Please forgive her, nurse. After all, she is the first woman *ever* to give birth."

Destiny shot her assistant a look that would've made Linda Blair proud, then tore off the light blanket covering the lower half of her body and kicked it onto the floor. The nurse scampered out of the room and went to locate the doctor.

"Where's Mike?!" she panted, wishing she'd made the time to attend Lamaze classes. Maybe there was a breathing exercise that could ease this hell.

"I called him, he's on his way," Chelsea said patiently. "The man does work, you know. And if you don't start behaving yourself I guarantee it'll be in the papers tomorrow."

"Do I look like I care!" she yelled, whimpering as the baby began to crown. "Oh, God! Oh, God! Chelsea, I have to push!"

"I guess you can kiss that epidural bye-bye, then!"

"Excuse me, my wife's having a baby—what floor is she on?" asked a harried Mike still in uniform, Ramirez trailing behind him.

"L&D is on the fourth floor, officer. I can notify them that you're on your way upstairs. What's your wife's name?"

"Destiny—uh, Mrs. Reilly!" he yelled over his shoulder as he charged through an exit door and took the stairs two at a time.

Ramirez, blew air through his teeth and gave the nurse a look as he pressed the elevator button. "New fathers!"

A nurse grabbed Mike by the hand and ran with him to the delivery room. He made it just in time to see his baby girl enter the world in a gush of amniotic fluid. The doctor cut the umbilical cord and a nurse placed the bawling infant on Destiny's chest. Mike gazed at her apologetically, his eyes full of tears and words he couldn't say. His daughter's birth was the most beautiful thing he had ever witnessed.

***

Mike let down the rail and gave Destiny a kiss that was so tender it made the attending nurse sigh.

"Careful, officer. That's how we ended up here in the first place," Destiny murmured with a weary smile. Mike made her feel like a heroine in some paperback novel. Even in that ugly hospital gown, with her mussed hair, aching breasts and neatly stitched bottom. She'd taken a nap after giving birth and was finally ready to see their baby. She'd promised her lactation consultant that she would make an attempt to breastfeed, but she wasn't really up to it. Hopefully they'd allow her to just pump the stuff and bottle feed the kid without too much fuss. The nurse helped prop Destiny up in the bed and then carefully placed a neatly wrapped bundle in her arms.

The first thing she noticed was Mike's aquamarine eyes staring back at her, then a cute little button nose, rosebud mouth and head full of dark brown curls. Destiny marveled at her tiny, shell-like ears and perfectly formed hands, toes and nails. So, this was who had given her heartburn for the past four months! Destiny was amazed and waited eagerly for the wave of love to wash over her that she'd heard so many new mothers speak of. But it didn't happen. She was fascinated, she was glad it was over, but she definitely wasn't in love. She wondered if that made her a bad mother.

"What's her name?" she asked softly, still staring at the quiet little stranger in her arms.

"Just *Baby Reilly* for now," Mike replied. "What would you like to call her?"

"I don't know. We looked at all of those names in that book—didn't you see any you liked?"

"How about Kayla? That one was pretty."

"Too popular."

"What about Laura?"

"Too *Little House*. I'm thinking something that brings water to mind—you know, for her eyes."

"Ariel?"

Destiny gave him a withering look. "You've been watching way too much Disney Channel. I've got it! How about *Marina*?"

"You want to name our firstborn after a place where boats pull in for repairs? You're joking, right?"

"No. What's wrong with it? It's pretty and it's got an oceany sort of feel to it. What do you think?" she asked with a slight frown.

"That we need to look through that book of names again."

In the end they agreed on the name *Ulla*, after Mike's grandmother. It was Celtic for sea jewel, which suited their new baby girl perfectly.

Chapter 21

Destiny gazed down into her daughter's crib and gently stroked the silky brunette curls on the baby's head. This small miracle which she and Mike had created was such a good, sweet-natured baby; she didn't even cry unless she was hungry or needed a diaper change, almost as though she sensed how disturbing the noise would be to her mother. When they had first brought her home from the hospital weeks ago, Ulla had bawled her head off and Destiny would immediately hand her over to Mike, or the nanny. Obviously their little girl was a quick study. Now she simply watched Destiny with those big aqua eyes and kept the ruckus down to a bare minimum.

Secretly, Destiny was grateful for the new nanny, whom Chelsea had interviewed and hired when Destiny began her third trimester. Changing poopy diapers and cleaning up regurgitated formula was not her cup of tea. Destiny already missed going out, wearing her designer clothes and the flash of media cameras in her face. Lately it had even made her depressed. She was bored staying at home and could hardly wait to get back into the swing of things. She often wondered how ordinary women did it, day in and day out. Babies were extremely demanding and—in Destiny's opinion—the occasional toothless smile wasn't compensation enough.

"Morning, beautiful," Mike whispered from behind her, enveloping her in his strong embrace.

Destiny leaned back into the warmth of his body and sighed contentedly. She was adoring her husband again. Funny, how being able to fit back into her favorite pair of skinny jeans and Jimmy Choos did for her libido. (Not to mention a recent shopping spree at Prada and Gucci.)

"Morning yourself, Officer Reilly," she purred, as he nuzzled the side of her neck. "What are you doing up?"

"Looking for you…why don't you come back to bed?" he asked.

"So that you can have your way with me?" she playfully

replied, turning in his arms to face him.

"Oh, yeah," he replied with a dimpled, minty smile.

Destiny wrapped her arms around his neck and began kissing him, but just when things were getting interesting the baby began to cry.

It was like someone threw ice water on Destiny. She bellowed for the nanny and stormed out of the nursery.

Mike picked the baby up and comforted her, his anxious gaze on his wife's retreating back. He handed Ulla to her caregiver as soon as she entered the room and raced down the hallway.

"Where are you going?" he asked, shutting the door to the master bedroom.

Destiny was getting dressed at a record speed. "Shopping."

"You just went shopping two days ago," he frowned.

She paused and looked at him pointedly, "I *need* to go again."

"You mean you *need* to get away from here, don't you?" Mike pressed, suspecting the truth.

"You always were one smart cookie, Officer Reilly," she smiled halfheartedly as she shimmied into a pair of Baby Phat jeans.

"You just need some time to adjust to parenthood. Shopping's not going to fix things," he said, gently grasping her shoulders to keep her still.

It was on the tip of Destiny's tongue to remind her husband that she hadn't wanted to be a mother in the first place, but something inside of her didn't want to hurt him. Mike adored his baby girl and she respected that. Just like he was going to have to respect the fact that she was about to head out that door and go buy herself something overpriced and sparkly.

"Talk to me, honey," he insisted.

"I'm taking a couple of the building's security team with me and the Town Car. I'll be back in a little while."

"Destiny—"

"No," she said firmly, holding up one hand like a traffic cop. "You've got Bible study and I've got Van Cleef & Arpels. Let's just leave it at that."

By the time Destiny returned it was almost nine p.m. She had been gone for nearly 12 hours. Mike had already gone to work and come back home, but he had checked in with the nanny during the course of the day. He was so angry he couldn't even speak when his wife came breezing through the door, arms laden with expensive purchases. The way she blew through money was disgraceful and irresponsible.

"Hey, handsome!" she grinned, throwing perfumed arms around his neck.

Mike studiously ignored her and changed the channel with the remote.

"I found the most incredible outfit for that upcoming charity affair! Wanna see it?"

"Not really." He stood up and went to the hallway closet to get his jacket.

"What's going on?"

"I need to get some fresh air."

"But I just got home," she said despondently.

"Who's fault is that?"

Destiny didn't reply. She was in a great mood and Mike wasn't. He would probably be back to his old self in the morning. She wasn't going to worry about it.

"Just an FYI: Terri's already fed Ulla and put her to bed. So you'll have plenty of free time to look through your purchases undisturbed."

"Where are you going?"

"Obviously not Van Cleef & Arpels. See you later," he said coolly, as he walked out the front door...

Chapter 22

The following weekend Destiny raced into the master bedroom and pounced on the bed. "Mike, wake up!" she said excitedly shaking her husband.

"What's wrong?" he asked, rousing almost immediately.

"Nothing's wrong—I have to tell you something!"

"You're up early, what's going on?" Mike said, scrubbing the sleep away from his eyes with the heel of one hand and glancing at the fancy porcelain and brass clock on her nightstand. It was eight o'clock on a Saturday morning.

"I was just on the phone with my agent! I've got incredible news...and not so incredible news. Which do you want first?" Destiny asked.

"You choose," he said patiently, wondering why her news couldn't wait until after he had brushed his teeth and had a decent cup of coffee.

"Remember the movie role I auditioned for while I was pregnant?"

"Yeah, vaguely. Something about a psychological thriller."

"That's the one! Well, my agent just called and told me that I got the part!"

"Wow! Congrats—that *is* incredible news."

"Well, before you get too happy for me, here's the downside: they're scheduled to start shooting soon."

"How soon?" he asked sitting up in the bed.

Destiny took a deep breath. "One month."

"You're kidding, right?" he asked deadpan.

"No. I wish I were."

"And I suppose they want you to fly out to Hollywood or something?"

She nodded her head, chewing her bottom lip.

"For how long, Destiny?"

"Four months tops. It's not the lead, it's a supporting role, so it shouldn't take long, but it's a huge opportunity, Mike! It can be difficult for recording stars to break into the film industry."

"You really want this?" he asked with a raised eyebrow. Her excitement was an almost tangible thing like it was that night at the awards show.

"You *know* I do! Please say that you're behind me on this," she pleaded with those sultry eyes that took his breath away.

"Ulla's not even six months old, Destiny…"

"I know," she sighed. "But we've got the nanny—"

"She's not supposed to be a substitute for our baby's real mother," Mike replied, secretly hating her career choices.

"It's just for a little while."

"I don't know, Destiny."

"I'll be back before you know it," she cajoled.

"You'd better be. Don't make me have to put out an APB on you!" he finally relented, though an uneasiness had settled over him that he couldn't shake.

***

On a chilly day in January, Mike didn't even have the pleasure of taking his wife to the airport. A limo picked Destiny and her entourage up and took them to JFK, where they boarded a rented Gulfstream G650. Destiny planned on making a grand entrance to LAX and arriving on a commercial airline—even first class—was out of the question. The crew personally greeted them on the tarmac and took care of their luggage and an attendant handed each of them glasses of Moët as they boarded. The pilot came out and welcomed them on board and the co-pilot gave them a tour of the private jet.

"Now this is classy!" Chelsea declared as she dug into her perfectly prepared filet mignon. "A girl could get used to this."

Destiny grinned and sipped her drink. She was too excited to talk or eat. An exciting new chapter in her life was about to begin! She gazed appreciatively around the rich interior of the cabin and then out a window at a clear cobalt sky high above the clouds.

Someone had once told her that she was so talented, the sky was the limit for her—man, if they could see her now!

Chapter 23

"Brace yourself. I've got bad news," Chelsea said with an expression that made the tiny hairs on the back of Destiny's neck rise. It reminded her of the time when there had been water damage from a burst pipe at her favorite designer's shop and she'd been left scrambling to find something Red Carpet worthy to wear to the BET Awards.

"What's going on?"

"Remember the actor who's supposed to play your love interest?"

"Yeah, that Australian hottie—what about him?"

"Well he got injured skiing in Aspen and he's going to be in the hospital for a little while."

"How much of a *little while*?"

"Probably a few months."

"Oh, no, Chelsea! Are the producers willing to wait, maybe shoot around him?"

"Uh, uh. They've got investors breathing down their necks as it is since they're already a couple of weeks behind schedule. They're replacing him."

"With who?"

"That's the bad news—"

A sudden knock on the door of Destiny's trailer interrupted them. She went to open it and felt her heart sink. This must have been the bad news Chelsea was referring to. *People* magazine's *Sexiest Man Alive*, Destiny's ex, was standing there on the steps, flashing his infamous smile…

"There is no way in hell I'm working with *that* man!" Destiny fumed.

"I don't blame you, girlfriend. Lord knows he's nothing but trouble. But keep in mind that you already signed on the dotted line. The studio practically owns you for however long it takes to market, make and release this movie. You back out now and you're asking for a whole lot of career and legal woes."

"Chelsea, the thought of him touching me is enough to make me sick."

"Well then, you'd better fake your way through those love scenes! If there was ever a time you have to be professional and bite the bullet, it's now, because Todd Hamilton isn't going anywhere."

"Ugh! Why did *he* have to be their first choice?" she asked pacing frantically.

"Actually, their first choice got broken up sliding down the side of some mountain, remember? Who knows how Hamilton found out about any of this! Whatever you decide, I have your back. You know that."

"I know. Thanks. At least I didn't have to find out about this last minute switch through social media."

"Eavesdropping at the water cooler pays off sometimes, doesn't it?" Chelsea reflected. "He certainly didn't waste any time getting down here, did he?"

Destiny groaned, the beginnings of a headache in her foreseeable future. "I need to hear Mike's voice. Can you give me a moment?"

"Sure, but just to warn you, the studio's having a dinner party tonight at some snooty restaurant to show off their latest acquisition."

"Great. I'll be there with bells on," Destiny said with a grimace.

***

"You look ravishing as always," Todd said with a kiss on Destiny's cool cheek. "Marc Jacobs?"

"Wouldn't you like to know," she shot back sweetly, as a photographer snapped their picture.

"Care to dance?"

"Not particularly," she replied, annoyed that he knew from a glance who had designed her LBD. He probably knew who had designed the shoes as well. She excused herself from the others at their table and escaped into the ladies' room. Fifteen minutes

98

later when she stepped into the hallway, Todd was there, leaning against a wall, a lit cigarette in his hand, despite the fact that no smoking was allowed.

"I know that you hate me—" he began.

"You have *no* idea."

"And you have every right to, but we're going to be working together for the next few months. We have to be civil to one another."

"I don't *have* to do a thing," she corrected, but as she went to walk past him Todd blocked her.

"No, you don't. But hear me out, anyway. We've got a hit on our hands, Destiny and you know I'm never wrong about a film. Hate me all you want, but use that anger, use the hurt! Put all that emotion into your acting. Don't let this opportunity slip through your fingers because of our history."

"Thanks for the advice. Am I free to go now?" she asked frostily.

Todd smiled knowingly and stepped aside. As she brushed past him he recognized the scent she was wearing. He was the one who had introduced her to it. He inhaled deeply, predatorily.

It was nice to know that some things never changed.

***

"So what's the movie about?" Dave asked, as he inhaled a third slice of pizza.

"It's a psychological thriller. That's all I know," Mike replied, as he opened the front door of his apartment.

"Man, if my woman was in another state making a movie, I'd know a whole lot more than you do! Did you know that they used to be involved?"

"What do you mean?"

"I mean they were like J. Lo and Ben back in the day! There was talk of an engagement for a minute, but he kept messing around with his leading ladies. Don't you watch *Entertainment Tonight*?"

"No and you shouldn't either. Don't believe everything you hear or read, Ramirez." Both men looked up at the sound of muffled footsteps entering the room.

"Oh, hello, Mr. Reilly. I didn't hear you come in. I just put the baby down for her nap."

"Terri, this is my partner, Dave Ramirez. Dave, Teresa Santiago, our nanny."

"Nice to meet you," she said with a warm smile as she shook his hand.

"Believe me, the pleasure is all mine," Dave replied with a lopsided grin. He'd always been a fool for a pretty Latina with curves and this one was no exception.

"Would you gentlemen like something to drink?"

"No thanks, Terri. Why don't you take it easy? I'll grab a couple of cans from the fridge."

"Alright. Take care, Officer Ramirez."

Dave watched as she walked down the hallway to her room. "You've got a *nanny*."

"Yeah. It was Destiny's idea."

"A nanny who lives with you," his partner mused.

"Get your mind out of the gutter, Ramirez."

"You're telling me you're never tempted?"

"I'm married—remember? And Terri's a pretty girl, but she's not Destiny."

"*Nobody's* Destiny. That's one hard act to follow."

Mike turned the television on and was surprised to see the subject of their conversation's face staring back at them. Some program was showing old footage of Destiny out on the town with a star that Mike recognized from a recent action blockbuster. Then they were interviewing the actor about the new film he was co-starring with Destiny in. Something about the man when he spoke about her turned Mike's stomach. He couldn't quite put his finger on it.

"I know that women go crazy over that guy, but I don't like him," Ramirez said.

"So it's not just me."

"I'm no saint, but he treats women like crap and he thinks he's God's gift to the gender."

Mike was quiet, but his partner could tell that his mind was working.

Dave just stared with a raised eyebrow. "Still not curious about that movie she's starring in?"

"It's just a job, Ramirez."

"So you're not the least bit concerned?"

"What are you saying?"

"If you've got any vacation time left you should use it, my friend. I would."

Chapter 24

"You'd better watch yourself out there," Chelsea warned.

Destiny rolled her eyes and pretended to busy herself with some things on her dressing table. "I don't know what you're talking about."

"Yeah, you do."

"Chelsea, don't start…"

Her assistant went and stood directly in front of her, then pinned her with a knowing look. "The cameras had stopped rolling today, the director had yelled 'cut!' and the two of you were still going at it like a couple of horny teens! I read the script—that scene didn't need to be *that* hot!"

"We just got caught up in the moment. Will you relax? I know what I'm doing!"

"I don't think you do. Maybe you were right, maybe this wasn't such a good idea after all."

Ignoring her, Destiny began vigorously brushing her hair. "So what are you suggesting that I back out now? What about that long speech you gave me a couple of months ago about biting the bullet and being professional?"

"That was before I realized that you still have a thing for your ex," Chelsea said astutely.

"No, I don't!" Destiny quickly replied.

"Oh, yes, you do! Look, you two have a history. You were practically engaged! Maybe you can get your lawyer to cry breach of contract or something. I have a bad feeling about this and you know my instincts are never wrong!"

"Relax, Chelsea. Nothing's going to happen. Like I said, we just got caught up in the moment."

"As long as he doesn't get caught up in anything else," Chelsea muttered. "When was the last time you spoke to your husband?"

"You are so in my business right now. You know that don't you?"

"That's what you pay me to do and don't think you're

getting out of answering my question."

"A couple of days ago, okay? It's been hectic on the set with them changing locations and all."

"Don't forget what you've got waiting for you at home."

"I know that you won't let me. Now, if you've finished lecturing, I'm going to have to throw you out."

"Why? Where are you going?"

"If you must know, a few of the cast members got invited to a party in the Hills."

"Does that *few* include Todd Hamilton?" Chelsea asked narrowing her eyes.

"We *are* the stars of this film."

"Just remember you have to be on the set at five a.m."

"I'll try to keep that in mind."

"And that you're married."

"I know that you won't let me forget," Destiny said sweetly, as she closed the trailer door behind her assistant.

***

"Where's the Porsche?" Destiny asked settling into the passenger seat.

"At home. Why, don't you like the Diablo? It's new," Todd said absently, watching her fasten the seatbelt. It was a treat just to look at her. She was wearing a body-skimming, Stella McCartney dress and Liz Palacios chandelier earrings. "You look incredible. Red always was your color."

"Thanks. Can you take me back to my hotel now?"

"Curfew?"

"I'm just tired, Todd. It's been a long day, you know." The truth was that all of it was feeling too familiar, too cozy and it made her uneasy. Todd had been by her side the entire evening and quite a few of the guests at the party were wondering if they were working on a relationship sequel. It probably wasn't the smartest decision on her part to go riding off into the night with him in his latest expensive toy. The rumor mill was probably churning at that very moment.

"Your wish is my command, gorgeous!"

When they got back to the hotel, Todd insisted on escorting Destiny upstairs.

"I'll be fine from here," she said opening the door with an access card.

"Not going to invite me in for a nightcap?" he asked with the smirk that had teenage girls plastering his picture on bedroom walls in the U.S. and overseas.

"I don't think that would be wise. Thanks for the ride."

"You're welcome. I'll see you in the morning, then. Have a good one, gorgeous."

"Good night, Todd," she said closing the door in his face. She leaned her back against it and noticed for the first time that she was trembling.

Chapter 25

Mike tip-toed across the living room floor and turned the entertainment center equipment off. As usual, a *Baby Einstein* DVD was playing. Terri had fallen asleep on the sofa with Ulla in her arms. He was about to wake her when something made him pause. It was the way they were holding one another, with so much trust and tenderness. It almost made his heart break. As far as his daughter was concerned Terri was mommy. Hollywood had called and Destiny had hit the ground running; they were lucky if they heard from her even once a week now. Mike fought back a familiar wave of resentment and then gently touched Terri's shoulder. She immediately woke up, apologetic.

"Mr. Reilly, I'm so sorry. I guess we dozed off while watching the DVD."

"It's okay. I'm glad you ladies were having a good time. Here, let me take her," he said reaching for the sleeping baby.

"Are you sure? I don't mind…"

"No, actually, I don't mind. I haven't seen my little princess since this morning. I'll tuck her in. Why don't you go get some rest?"

"Thanks, Mr. Reilly."

"And call me Mike—for the hundredth time—before I write you a ticket. I feel like you're addressing my grandfather, or something."

"Sorry about that…Mike. I'll see you in the morning."

When Mike returned from work that evening, he was greeted by an excited nanny and a happy gurgling baby. An almost perfect ending to his day.

"Wanna show your dad what you did today?" Terri asked Ulla. "Watch this, Mike," she said animatedly, gently holding the toddler's chubby hands.

Mike's eyes grew misty as he watched his daughter take her first unsteady steps towards him.

"Yea!" Terri exclaimed, clapping proudly when Ulla

landed on her diapered bottom.

Mike scooped his baby up and gave her kisses. "Is today the first time she did that?" he asked a bit wistfully.

"Yes, but don't despair!" Terri grinned, rushing over to the entertainment center and snatching up her cell phone. "All the firsts are getting recorded…so you won't miss a thing!"

"Terri, you're the best!" Mike declared. "I don't know how you find the time," he continued, "but, I'm grateful. Sometimes I feel as though I'm missing out on so much. I'm just glad you're here."

"I'm glad, too," Terri said with a smile. Ulla babbled and held out her arms to her nanny.

"I think she'd rather be with you," Mike laughed, handing the baby over.

"I think *somebody's* spoiled," Terri replied under her breath.

"And whose fault is that?"

"Not mine," Terri said innocently. "I'm just the nanny."

"That leaves my family," Mike said with a crestfallen expression.

"And?" she prodded.

"Ramirez and his family. It's got to end here."

"I agree," Terri said solemnly, trying not to laugh.

"You want ice cream?"

"I'd love some."

"So would the one in diapers," she confided. "Let's see what's in the freezer."

Chapter 26

The after-party at LA's hot new club, *Narcissist,* was in full swing by the time they arrived and everybody who was anybody had accepted the invitation to eat, drink and take merry to another level. Destiny glimpsed a couple of film/television stars here and there, but music industry's elite dominated the scene. Todd knew quite a few of them and Destiny couldn't help but feed into the excitement of it all. She barely noticed the photographer, who was trailing them, but Todd did and he smiled within himself. He took Destiny's hand and steered her through the throng to the VIP lounge upstairs, where he snagged two glasses of Cristal from a passing waitress.

"Having a good time, gorgeous?" he asked, clinking her glass with his.

"Yes. The energy here is unbelievable!" she said, taking a sip.

"I'm glad," he said, squeezing her waist. They sat down in a cozy, private area where the lighting was minimal, but a plate glass window afforded them a terrific view of the activity below.

"Who owns this place?"

"I do," he said, flashing a smile.

"Stop lying."

"Nightclubs are great investments. I thought it was time I got in on the action."

Staring at him boldly, Destiny cut to the chase. "Why are we here, Todd?"

"You know why we're here," he replied evenly.

"I declared a truce for the sake of the film. We're not an item any more."

"But you have to admit we were something when we were an item."

"Yes, we were *something*," she said, looking past him at the myriad of flashing lights and trying to forget the pain and humiliation he'd caused her.

"Destiny," he cajoled, lifting her chin with his hand. "I

blew it. I messed up. How many times do I have to say I'm sorry?"

She dared to glance at him, an odd combination of anxiety and yearning in her heart. What was it about Todd that made her knees quake and her judgment fly out a window? And where was her resolve when she needed it? He was nothing but another heartache waiting to happen. She had a family now and being within a five-mile radius of Todd Hamilton was like playing with fire.

Destiny started to rise and Todd beat her to the punch. "Let's dance, gorgeous, they're playing our song."

Sure enough, Mariah Carey's, *Don't Forget About Us*, was playing in the background and suddenly the dance floor was filled with couples swaying slowly.

"Todd—I can't," she said shakily, reaching for her beaded clutch.

"Can't what? Dance with an old friend? Please tell me that cop's not that insecure." He pulled Destiny's reluctant form into his arms and playfully dipped her. When he pulled her back up, their bodies collided and for the first time in her life she understood how things could sometimes just happen…

There was something different about them when they came back downstairs and the journalist suspected he knew what it was. He made sure to capture it on film.

A picture might be worth a thousand words…these were worth much more.

***

Destiny awoke the following morning with a start. Looking around the familiar black and chrome room, she held her head in her hands and groaned. She was at Todd's Malibu beach house…in his bed. She couldn't even remember the drive back to his place. The last thing she recalled was champagne flowing like a fountain and dancing to a remix of Britney Spears' old hit, *Baby One More Time*, which was exactly what the media would be screaming. She swung her legs over the side of the black platform bed and padded unsteadily to the floor-to-ceiling windows. Sure enough, Todd was already outside on the deck on his cell phone, wheeling and dealing with his agent about what script he'd be reading next, a cigarette in one hand and a double espresso in the other.

Oddly enough, a part of Destiny felt as though she had finally come full circle, but another part of her was extremely troubled. Panicking, she started gathering her things so that she could be dressed before Todd finished his call. She was on her knees looking for the mate to her Manolo Blahnik when she heard him clearing his throat.

"Morning, gorgeous. Leaving so soon?" he asked with a look that would've buckled her knees had she not already been down on them.

"I—I have to go. I shouldn't be here," she stammered, flabbergasted by the empty condom wrappers littering the floor.

Todd handed her the missing shoe.

He had Destiny right where he wanted her and had no intention of losing her again. Todd almost felt like kicking himself, because if he had been more discreet Destiny would still be with *him* and not legally bound to that nobody on the East Coast. The crucial thing to do at that juncture was to soothe her and no one knew how to do that better than he did.

He held out his hands to her. "Don't beat yourself up, gorgeous. We both had too much to drink last night and it just happened. Nobody planned it."

"I'm married, Todd! I can't allow things to *just happen*! I have to get out of here."

"Hey, slow down! Why don't you take a shower and have something to eat? I promise I won't lay a hand on you." *At least not until after my conference call at noon*, he chuckled inwardly.

That seemed to appease her and he could tell that she was weighing her options. "What am I supposed to wear when I get out of the shower?" she asked suspiciously. The thought of putting the little black dress on from the previous night made her skin crawl.

Todd grinned triumphantly. "Your clothes are still in that box in the guest room closet."

"Why?" she almost whispered.

"Just in case," he shrugged innocently. "I guess it's a good thing I held onto them."

***

It was on the front page of a major tabloid newspaper the very next day and splattered all over the internet. Destiny in the black D&G cutout dress, Todd in a black Versace suit and the glass of champagne they were sharing, along with some additional shots of them burning up the dance floor, canoodling by the bar and holding hands as they exited the club. The evidence was damning.

Destiny sat numbly in her monogrammed bathrobe, studiously avoiding Chelsea's glare. Somewhere in the haze of her emotions she thought she heard a phone ringing.

"Bill's on your cell."

"Thanks, I'll take it," Destiny murmured.

"And your boyfriend's on the hotel line."

The women's eyes met for the first time and the disapproval in the personal assistant's expression made the star glance away with shame. "Please…tell Todd that I'll call him back later."

"My pleasure."

Steeling herself, Destiny placed the cell phone against her ear. "Hi, Bill."

"Honey, I've got to tell you the D&G dress was all that, but, *what were you thinking?*"

"Apparently I wasn't," she replied so dryly she nearly choked.

"How do you want to handle this? You know I can weave a tale as long as a diva's extensions if necessary."

Destiny almost giggled. Almost. "I'm more concerned about Mike, than fans and the press right now. Just keep them at bay until I figure out what I'm going to say to my husband."

"Okay. I'll swear from here to Australia that nothing's going on. But be honest with me—*are* you and Todd together again?"

"No…no…oh, I don't know, Bill! I thought I was certain about everything in my life until last night happened."

110

The PR man sighed audibly. "No worries. Just make sure that you iron things out with your hubby. I'll take care of the rest! Smooches, honey."

"Smooches back at you and thanks, Bill."

Bill didn't want her thanks. What he wanted to do was tell her that he had already spoken with her agent that morning, who was secretly thrilled about what had happened. Searches for Destiny on the internet were unprecedented and her official fan site had crashed twice because of all of the hits. This little debacle of hers had probably only cost her a happy marriage.

Chapter 27

"What are you doing here, Todd? I told you I'd call you later," she hissed, scanning the hallway and then yanking him into her suite.

"That was three days ago. I just wanted to see how you were," he replied, noting the dark circles under her eyes. "I brought sustenance."

"I'm not hungry," she said ungraciously, as she rushed to close the drapes. That was all she needed, somebody with a high-powered lens snapping shots of Todd in her hotel suite.

"Why are you doing this to yourself?" he asked, setting the bag of gourmet goodies down on a coffee table.

"What are you talking about?" she asked irritably.

"Hiding out."

"*Hiding*? I'm hiding thanks to *you*! You know the way out," she said, turning to walk away, but Todd refused to be dismissed so easily.

He took her arm and spun her around. "This is who you are and where you belong! You're a *movie star* now, Destiny, not a housewife! So pull yourself together! That cop's never going to be able to relate to this lifestyle. We don't dream on the same level as ordinary people! Why don't you just tell him that you're not coming home and finish this already?"

Destiny drew in a sharp breath and then slapped Todd hard across the face. When his ears finally stopped ringing he gingerly touched his bruised cheek. He almost laughed out loud. That was a moment made in celluloid history! But there was a fearful look in her eyes that confirmed what he already knew. The two of them were unfinished business and she was fighting it.

Movie offers were pouring in left and right; studios were vying for the two of them. Todd could care less about her recording career. Hollywood was where Destiny belonged, in front of a camera and in his bed. He planned on keeping things that way.

Todd started walking away from her and then stopped

in his tracks. He didn't know why he found her so appealing—Hollywood was teeming with eager, beautiful women—maybe he just hated the idea of someone else owning something he'd always considered his in the first place. Whatever the reason, he walked back over to Destiny, pinned her against the wall and kissed her possessively.

"When you get a clue, you know how to reach me," he rasped, releasing her and slamming the front door behind him.

Destiny had no idea how long she hugged that wall, or when she actually began breathing normally again. All she knew was that as guilty as she felt, she wanted to run down that hotel hallway after Todd and the worst part about it was he knew it, too.

***

The clandestine product of a South African movie star and married, affluent British film producer, Todd Hamilton was just another piece of eye candy when he was discovered. His father called in a couple of favors and the next thing Todd knew he was reading for some hot shot producer and a supporting role in a major summer blockbuster was his. After all was said and done, Todd turned out to be a 'natural' and to everyone's surprise became an overnight success, especially with the 15- to 35-year old female demographic. He had charisma, sex appeal and *zero* competition in the good looks department. He was every director's dream: Todd consistently arrived at the set on time, did what he was told, and left his ego inside his trailer. As long as he steered clear of bad press the sky wasn't even the limit for him.

One weekend while on location in the Big Apple, Todd was invited by some acquaintances to a show at Radio City Music Hall. He couldn't even recall who was headlining, but he remembered the opening act—some gorgeous number with streaked honey-colored hair and a set of pipes that could blow right through you. He'd never even heard of her since he wasn't into R&B, but he made it his business to find out everything he could about her before night's end and showed up at her dressing room door after the show with a bouquet of white calla lilies, her favorite flower…

They were the bicoastal IT couple for almost 24 months. Everywhere they went, everything they did, was gobbled up by the press. They were the ultimate hot commodity and the fans were panting for more. When Destiny went on tour to promote a new CD, Todd was guaranteed to be backstage—and when he was starring in a new movie she was guaranteed to be on the set, or waiting for him in his trailer. It was a match made in tabloid heaven until Todd began to get bored—not so much with Destiny, per se, as being in a monogamous relationship. Things continued to go downhill when one tabloid, in particular, started the engagement rumor. Todd might have married Destiny... eventually. She was a knockout and he was crazy about her, but he had just turned thirty and wasn't even thinking about the ultimate commitment. Needless to say that Destiny grew tired of his philandering ways, especially after she'd found his latest conquest's underwear in her laundry hamper.

Todd had kept tabs on Destiny, however, and watched as her star continued to climb until she crossed over from music to film. As soon as he'd heard about her co-star being out of commission he'd told his agent to get him the part or find a new job.

Destiny was on the cusp of superstardom and he wanted in on the action. He also wanted her back in his life and could care less about her so-called marriage. He knew Destiny better than that cop did. Knew what drove her, what her dreams were, what excited her. He knew the side of her that was determined to have it all no matter the cost and that was the part of her he was gunning for. Destiny was meant for the finer things in life. That's who she was. Todd couldn't begin to imagine her with a burp cloth covering the shoulder of a designer gown that was worth more than a cop's annual salary! A cop couldn't even afford a woman like Destiny! Her husband was completely out of his league.

Todd Hamilton wasn't concerned about who was on the East Coast or any other coast for that matter. He always got what he wanted and what he wanted now was his ex.

Chapter 28

Mike's flight to Los Angeles was a blur. All he could think about was Destiny's betrayal. He couldn't sleep or eat; he just felt numb. And it seemed as though every tabloid in the nation was covering the story. He even noticed a couple of wide-eyed stewardesses gawking at him and whispering.

He had never felt so hurt and humiliated in his entire life.

Overnight Destiny had turned him into an object of ridicule and pity…and yet, he didn't hate her. He didn't know if he'd ever be able to forgive her, but he didn't hate her. In fact, he still loved her so much it made his chest hurt.

Mike replayed the events over and over again in his mind trying to make sense of it all, trying to figure out who was to blame. And it always came back to him. He knew better than to get involved with an unsaved woman. He'd left a door wide open and the enemy had stampeded right through it. Imps and all.

Destiny paced the hotel room floor. Hotel security had just phoned her. Mike was downstairs. She gave them permission to send him up, even though her entire body was trembling with apprehension.

She wrung her hands and repeatedly checked the door's peephole. She knew that he was coming to Los Angeles to talk, thanks to an abrupt phone call she had received from him a couple of days ago, but of all days for him to show up! She had to go out that night to promote the movie—the entire cast did. She didn't want to, knew it was the worst possible timing, but she had no say in the matter. Now here she stood, looking like she was ready to party and not the least bit concerned about her personal life.

There was a sudden sharp knock on her door.

Woodenly, she made her way over to it, unlocked it, and turned the handle with a shaky hand. Destiny just wanted to tell Mike that she was sorry, beg him not to hate her. But, the minute she looked into her husband's eyes all hope was lost.

She must have been getting ready to go to yet another

awards show, because she was Red Carpet ready that evening. She was wearing a gold Elie Saab gown that left just enough to the imagination, coordinating Jimmy Choos and a Harry Winston pin in her chignon that could probably lease a third world country.

Mike almost laughed out loud. He still couldn't believe that he was actually married to her. It was like some great big cosmic joke…only, it wasn't funny. He wished for a moment that she wasn't the mother of his child; it would have made it easier for him to forget about her. He glanced at her left hand and noted that her engagement ring and wedding band were missing. There was, however, a stunning diamond and gold cocktail ring gracing the ring finger on her right hand, which complimented her gown.

Why was he not surprised?

The woman had allowed him to find out about her indiscretion through the media! She hadn't even had the decency to call him before it hit the newsstands and internet. He'd had to contact *her* to officially call it quits. As far as Mike was concerned, that alone made her less than human.

Destiny parted her lips to speak and Mike flung the newspapers and magazines at her feet, startling her back into silence.

Everything within him felt bruised and betrayed and he finally understood why people committed crimes of passion. If he was a violent man he would have slapped her. She looked uncertain and frightened by his actions and he had no intention of easing her conscience. Not when they had a baby girl at home who this was going to hurt the most.

How could she just throw it all away, like they were garbage? As if they had no value? He'd rather for her to shoot him than do what she'd done. Mike could almost hear Ramirez warning him not to marry her, his pastor advising him to pray first. It had all been one big mistake, even if his heart wanted to argue the point.

Destiny didn't move a muscle—the man's nostrils were flaring and his eyes were a stormy teal framed with dark circles. She'd been fooling herself. There wouldn't be a calm, rational discussion about what had happened. So far, he hadn't breathed a word… she'd never seen him like this. She had also been foolish to think that she could have a normal life. That she could be the sort of wife and mother her family deserved. She wanted desperately to talk with Mike, but fear and uncertainty had immobilized her. For the space of four heartbeats the silence in the room was deafening.

When Mike finally spoke, it was in a condemning voice that she didn't even recognize. "I couldn't understand why God didn't want me to be with the woman I loved. Couldn't understand why He kept warning me about you—but, unfortunately, I get it now. You don't care about anybody but yourself, Destiny. You have no idea what it means to lay your life down for someone you love, to put someone else's needs first. You act first and let the chips fall wherever they want and you could care less about where they fall, or who they land on. I gave you my heart and a beautiful baby girl…that should have meant something to you."

Destiny watched, dumbfounded, as Mike turned away and walked out of her life.

***

"Miss me, gorgeous?" Todd asked, watching her with shrewd eyes as she entered his lavish home. A mole had informed him that she'd had a visit from the cop, so he already knew that she was on edge and needed to be handled with kid gloves.

"You did tell me to contact you when I got a clue…didn't you?" she solemnly replied, as she walked over to his well-stocked bar and placed an expensive cabernet sauvignon on the counter.

"And have you?"

"I'm here, aren't I?"

Todd put the bottle back in the fridge beneath the counter. "I don't want a repeat performance of that first night we hooked up. If you want to be with me you're going to have to do it without this."

Destiny was trembling inside. She felt like she was digging her own grave.

Why was she really there?

She should be home, down on her knees, begging Mike for his forgiveness.

Todd was looking at her expectantly, his intention clear in his obsidian eyes.

It would be so easy to just forget New York and everything that had happened there and slip back into a lifestyle she was accustomed to. Forget the accusing look in Mike's eyes, the chill in his voice and the child she had left behind.

If only she could forget. She had a feeling that she never would and at that moment she felt so cold, lonely, and ashamed. She just needed someone to hold her, to warm her for just a little while.

She fought back tears, as she slipped into Todd's welcoming arms.

Tonight painful memories would be put on hold.

Tomorrow was another story.

Chapter 29

Mike stood in front of his locker, staring numbly at the tabloid photos of Destiny taped on its front door. The word *sucker* was written on one and *you got played* on another. He refused to look at the others.

He slammed his fist into the door, as angry tears filled his eyes. He'd hoped that his brothers in blue would at least have his back, but some of them were right up there with Judas. Destiny was still the mother of his child and she deserved respect for that if nothing else.

He swung around, determined to confront his fellow officers after roll call and almost collided with Ramirez. His partner took one glance at the locker and shook his head angrily. He tore the photos down and gave Mike a hard look. "Some of these guys were jealous from day one. Just let it go. You go off during roll call and you're gonna make a bad situation worse."

"What am I supposed to do, Ramirez? She's still the mother of my kid."

"I know. You'd think the idiot would at least respect that."

"Do you know who's doing it? This isn't the first time," Mike said, his voice filled with frustration.

"I've got a hunch. Let me handle this."

"This is my problem—"

"No. When they messed with you they made it *our* problem. We're partners, remember?"

Ramirez waited patiently until the end of their shift. He knew exactly who the culprit was because the person had been pretty opinionated about Mike's marriage from the start, especially after a couple of beers. While others had been congratulatory that one cop had kept his distance and Ramirez noted the look of envy in his eyes on more than one occasion.

As the officers swarmed into the locker room to gather their things and call it a night, Ramirez went to stand in front of the suspected cop's locker. He was just a dumb kid, but tonight he was going to learn a valuable lesson about loyalty and respect. Some of the more seasoned cops had seen the look on Ramirez's face before and gave him a wide berth. The rookie had no idea about what was coming and nobody was going to warn him.

"Yo, Ramirez—"

The punch to the rookie's gut happened so fast a couple of the officers watching weren't certain they'd actually seen it. While the rookie was doubled over and gasping for air Ramirez grabbed him by the collar and forced him to look up. "A couple of things we don't tolerate in this house are rats and disrespectful punk rookies! That was just a taste of what you'll be getting if you feel the urge to stick anything else on my partner's locker."

Ramirez cracked his knuckles and walked out of the locker room, glad that he had sent Reilly to the deli a couple of blocks away for something to eat. No one would ever be able to say that Mike had anything to do with this. Not that anyone would. As far as Ramirez was concerned Mike didn't ever have to know why the photos of Destiny stopped showing up on his locker. That's just what good partners were for.

***

The walk to the deli helped Mike clear his head. In spite of everything, he was grateful for his job. When all else failed, there were still plenty of bad guys to arrest, tickets to write, and doughnuts to be consumed. Or so he thought, until he returned to the precinct and had to battle his way through a horde of journalists, hungry for his side of the story. Mike tried to be as polite as possible, but he was annoyed that they had found out where he worked and some of their questions were rude and offensive. He was about to swing on one journalist in particular, when he felt someone grab his arm. Ramirez gave him a look, and motioned with his head for Mike to go inside. A few other officers came outside and quickly sent the disappointed journalists packing. Unfortunately, Mike's captain heard about what happened and called him into his office.

"You wanted to see me, Captain?" Mike asked after knocking on his superior's open door.

"Come in and have a seat, Reilly."

Mike sat down in a dark brown leather chair in front of his mentor's desk and waited patiently for the older man to speak.

"You're one the best officers on the force, Reilly. I've always said so and I believe that you're going to go far in the law enforcement field."

"Thank you, sir."

The captain held up a hand. "You might want to hold off on thanking me. There's no reason to beat around the bush about this. I'm recommending some time off for you, Reilly."

Mike was speechless, although he should have expected this. His personal life was a shambles; he hadn't been at the top of his game for weeks.

"This is a precinct, son. We're in the business of putting miscreants behind bars…not putting up with the press camping out on our doorstep. Get your personal affairs in order and then contact HR in a few weeks."

"Does Ramirez know about this, Captain?"

"Nobody does," the older man muttered. "And I'm not looking forward to hearing your partner's mouth when he does hear about it."

"Will that be all, Sir?" Mike asked rising slowly from his seat, not sure whether to be grateful or upset about the mandatory leave.

"That'll be all."

Mike started for the door, wondering what he was going to do with all the free time he had just been allotted. Sitting at home and brooding about his imminent divorce was definitely out of the question.

"Reilly," his superior said stopping him in his tracks.

"Yes, Captain?"

"Sorry to hear about what happened with Destiny. Give Ulla a hug and kiss from me and the missus."

"Will do. Thank you, Sir."

"Don't mention it. I expect to see you back on the job soon and so will Ramirez…God help us."

Chapter 30

Mike's family wanted to see him. Since returning from California and his forced leave of absence from work, he had kept to himself. When a month had passed without a word from him, his mother was threatening to go over to his place. So finally, one night, he bundled Ulla up warmly, secured her in the car seat and drove over to his family's house.

When he pulled into the driveway, he sighed heavily. He gazed up at his childhood home, a charming Tudor, boasting two fireplaces, five bedrooms and two and a half baths. It still retained the original stained-glass windows and French doors from its youth, as well as a new gazebo and cast-iron bistro set his mother had recently purchased to compliment the rose garden she took such meticulous care of.

Destiny hadn't appreciated any of it—this place so full of love, warmth, and good memories. It had probably seemed small and dull and ordinary to someone like her.

Mike felt his heart breaking all over again, as he climbed slowly out of his vehicle and went to get his baby and the diaper bag out of the back seat.

His mother was already waiting for him by the front door. His sister took the sleeping baby and the diaper bag and left the two of them alone. The minute Mike's mother cupped her son's face in her hands, he broke down. She hugged him tightly. Her head barely reached his shoulders, but the strength and love emanating from her was enough to fortify her firstborn. She continued to hold him, making soothing noises just as she had done when consoling him as a small child. When he finally stopped crying, she took him by the hand into the kitchen and gently pushed a large mug of hot chocolate in front of him.

"Do you know why we named you Michael?" she asked rhetorically. "Because from the moment we laid eyes on you we knew that you were a warrior, a leader, even though you came early and the doctors were saying all kinds of negative things

122

about your chances of survival. You were such a beautiful baby. I knew that God, Himself, had hand delivered you to us. So we gave you a powerful name—a name to be reckoned with! Michael, the Archangel. You're in a battle, but you're not alone. You have the prayers and support of all who love you and you're going to come through this stronger and wiser...even if it doesn't feel like it right now."

Mike looked gratefully at his mom. "Thanks for not saying *I told you so.*"

"How could those words encourage anyone?" she asked, shaking her head. "Leave the baby with us whenever you need a breather. She'll be safe here. You know that."

Mike nodded his head solemnly.

"A better day's coming, Mikey. That much I promise you."

"Thanks, Ma."

"You're welcome, son. Now, drink the rest of your cocoa before it gets cold!"

Mike's sister opened the door to the nursery. Ulla was fast asleep in an oval-shaped antique crib. Brother and sister stood side by side gazing down at the slumbering child.

"She's beautiful, Mike."

"Thanks, Sis, and thanks for all of this," he said, gesturing gratefully around the former guest room.

His sister beamed. She and their mom had a terrific time choosing the perfect pieces of furniture at Bellini's and picking out the antique sage, rose, and cream bedding and matching accessories. The family adored their newest addition—didn't feel that way about Destiny, but the baby they were over the moon about. "You're welcome. She's so worth it...both of you are." She gave her older brother a spur-of-the-moment hug. "I love you," she whispered.

"I know, pip squeak," Mike said, ruffling the top of her hair with his knuckles. "The feeling's mutual."

"So, what's the game plan?"

"Don't have one yet."

"You know you guys are welcome to stay here—there's plenty of room."

"I know. Mom already told me. I'm going to look for a new place, though. Just not right this minute."

"You still got the nanny?"

"Yeah. She's been great."

"She's not family, though," his sister said with a sniff.

"No, she's not. But she's been very supportive and helpful."

"Is she willing to relocate when you find the new place?"

"That's a good question," Mike said thoughtfully, as he gently stroked his daughter's soft dark curls.

Chapter 31

"How are you doing, Mike?" the pastor asked, sitting down slowly in the pew beside him.

Mike snorted uncharacteristically and continued to stare at the podium. The words *Do This In Remembrance Of Me* were emblazoned in the wood. Something about the quiet splendor of the sanctuary had always given him peace. But today peace was an elusive thing. In his mind's eye he kept seeing those photos of his wife in another man's arms. He finally looked at his pastor, praying that he didn't look as lost as he felt. "You warned me about her."

"Actually, I advised you to seek the heart of the Father—"

"Because mine could lead me astray. You were right. Marrying Destiny was not one of the wisest choices I've made."

"We all make mistakes, Mike, but the good news is that this moment isn't going to last forever. You can learn from this experience, grow from it, and choose to make different choices because of it…instead of allowing heartache and disappointment to defeat, or consume you. Just showing up in God's house today—I'd say you're already making wiser choices."

"Thanks, Pastor Hammond," Mike murmured. "If only I'd kept my eyes on Him, the way He instructed me to…"

"Stop beating yourself up. Have you already prayed and asked the Lord to forgive you?"

"Yes, but—"

"No buts. Rest in Him, abide in Him, *trust* in Him. He's already working everything out for your good, Mike, no matter what it looks like. It's up to you to believe it. I'm not going to make light of what you're going through—I understand what it feels like to be hurting and wondering where God is when He promised us that He would never leave us or forsake us. The thing is: He *is* there, Mike. He's been there all along and He's not happy that you're suffering right now. He loves and cares about you, more than you'll ever know. Spend some time with Him. He said that He'll heal your broken heart and bind up your wounds and

He's given you a comforter who'll stick closer to you than a flesh and blood brother! If that doesn't sound inviting, I don't know what does…"

Mike stood up and gave his pastor a grateful look. He held out his hand for the older man to shake; the pastor ignored it. He gave the youth leader a warm, powerful hug instead and then quietly left the sanctuary.

Mike slowly made his way up to the altar and got down on his knees.

He knew that this battle wasn't over yet, not by a long shot.

But finally, he remembered, where he had to go to get the strength and courage to face it. At the foot of a cross and at the feet of his Savior.

Chapter 32

Destiny anxiously clutched Todd's hand as he helped her out of the limo. It was their first public appearance as a couple since her divorce and she had been dreading it for weeks. Todd, on the other hand, looked like a kid on Christmas morning. He had definitely gotten everything on his wish list.

"Smile, gorgeous—you're going to knock 'em dead," he whispered in her ear, as he snaked a possessive arm around her waist. Then he turned to face the sea of journalists and shrieking fans and gave them his infamous sexy smirk.

The female fans would have torn down the barricades were it not for the police; it was a wonder that they were able to keep the masses at bay. Destiny vaguely heard Todd say "no comment" to a couple of pushy reporters along the way. She kept an artificial smile plastered to her face and worked the Red Carpet like Hollywood royalty. The press gobbled it up and were, not surprisingly, more interested in the king's ransom in borrowed Neil Lane bling adorning the chanteuse's person than the fact that the ink was still drying on her divorce papers.

***

"I noticed you were speaking to that French director at the after-party," Todd commented, loosening his Armani tie.

Destiny slipped Christian Louboutin stilettos off her tired feet. "He wants me to star in an independent film he's working on next year."

"Really? Way to go, gorgeous!" Todd enthused until he noticed her face. "Why do I get the feeling you're not as excited as I am?"

"Because I got the feeling that he was interested in a lot more than my acting ability," she replied with a look of disgust.

"Who cares? The prestige and salary are worth it."

"*You* should care!" she said pointedly. "Sometimes you make Hollywood sound like a brothel, Todd."

"That's what it is," he replied, strolling up behind her and unzipping the back of her Versace gown. "I mean, think about it:

the right age, the right looks and talent to spare—you could sell yourself to the highest bidder!"

"And what are you, Todd? My pimp?" Destiny asked with distaste.

"If you want me to be," he half teased, kissing her bare shoulder.

Destiny pulled away. "I'm going to soak in the tub. It's been a long night."

Todd wore an easy-going smile that didn't quite reach his dark eyes. "Alright, I'll see you when you come out."

"Don't wait up," she coolly replied, as she retreated into a guest bathroom.

Destiny had been in the tub for over 30 minutes; she was still fuming when a sudden light tap on the door interrupted the moment.

"Can I come in?" Todd asked humbly.

Destiny had a few responses for that query—none of them were kind. "Sure," she finally replied, slipping farther beneath the scented bubbles. The last thing she wanted to do was let him think he was going to get lucky after his earlier comments.

"Truce?" he said, with puppy dog eyes and a crystal dish offering full of Belgian chocolate-covered strawberries that were usually a no-no in his house. Everything was usually organic, gluten and fat free and wouldn't tempt a starving man.

Obviously, he had figured out that he'd messed up big time. That was why he was standing beside the tub looking like he had just stepped out of a CK print ad.

A Hollywood icon and chocolate-covered fruit.

Who could ask for more?

Destiny almost forgot why she'd become so unhinged in the first place.

"White chocolate—" she murmured reverently, focusing her attention back on the array of delicacies.

"—dipped in crushed almonds."

She eyed Todd with new appreciation. "Get in," she commanded, reaching for the dish of goodies.

128

"Thought you'd never ask," he said with a grin, as he tore out of his navy silk lounge pants.

Destiny sighed. She definitely had a weakness for decadent sweets and hot men. Unfortunately, Todd knew it, too.

Later, a sated Todd smiled briefly in the darkness of his chrome and black bedroom, as Destiny slept beside him.

She was so easy. The way to her heart had always been through her stomach...

Some things really never changed.

***

"What's this?" Destiny asked, looking suspiciously at the envelope Chelsea handed to her the following morning after Todd had gone out.

"A letter of resignation," was Chelsea's solemn reply.

"Chelsea, you can't—don't do this to me!" she said in a panic.

"I enclosed a list of recommendations. You shouldn't have any problems finding someone new."

"Why are you doing this? *I need you!*" Destiny exclaimed.

"Like your family needed you?"

"You're taking this way too personally, Chelsea. You and I were a team long before Mike and I had anything going."

"How else am I supposed to take it? I arranged your first date with Mike, for crying out loud! Do you really believe that you're going to get a happily ever after ending with Todd Hamilton?"

"Things are different this time around. He's changed."

"No he hasn't! That man's a garden tool to his core! He was checking out your makeup girl the other day, for crying out loud!"

"That's not fair, Chelsea."

"Oh, wake up, Destiny! The man came looking for you and I'm sure that he pulled whatever strings necessary in order to be in that film. He's a user and a snake and he only cares about himself! Tell me something, has he asked even once to meet Ulla?"

"What kind of question is that?"

"Apparently one that you're not going to answer. If you weren't going to do the right thing by him, then you should have left Mike alone. He deserves better than this! Just remember that you reap what you sow."

"What's that supposed to mean?" Destiny asked sarcastically.

"You'd better start praying for a crop failure!"

Chapter 33

Months later, Mike was still living in Destiny's condo. It pained him daily to see so many reminders of her at every turn, but he simply hadn't the heart, or the energy to house hunt. He'd given up his apartment when he and Destiny wed and living with his family simply wasn't an option. He needed peace and quiet and to continue reconnecting with God. He still hadn't resumed serving in the ministry at his church, but at least he'd been going consistently and that was a start.

He was relaxing and listening to a Warren Hill CD on a breezy Saturday afternoon when he heard a knock at the door. Ulla was spending the weekend with his parents and Terri was visiting her sisters. Mike wasn't expecting anyone—security notified tenants about *every* guest, even maintenance people. Mystified, he gazed through the peephole and immediately stepped away from the door.

It was Destiny…

"I was in town on business and wanted to stop by to speak with you. Sorry about the surprise visit," she said quietly.

Mike's tongue felt like sandpaper. He hadn't uttered a word since allowing her inside.

"I want you to have the condo," she nervously continued. "You won't have to worry about rent or mortgage payments and I'll continue to cover any other expenses related to it. The media's going to be a nightmare for a while and you and Ulla will be safe here."

Mike stared at her with disbelief. Was this supposed to be compensation for his pain and suffering? *Was she for real?* "You think that I care about living arrangements right now?" he asked, finally finding his voice.

Destiny looked stricken. Tears threatened to roll down her cheeks, but she hurriedly wiped them away.

"Why, Destiny? Was it because he's a movie star?"

"Don't do this," she pleaded, defensively clutching her

favorite Juicy Couture bag. "That's not why I came here."

"Because he's rich?" he insisted, dogging her steps.

"Mike—"

"What was it, Destiny? *I need to understand!*"

"Just let it go!" she cried, whirling around to face him. "Don't you see? I don't have any answers for you! I just had to be free!"

"I love you...don't do this."

"I love you, too, but, don't try to stop me." She rushed over to the door, but ended up leaning her forehead against it and crying bitterly.

Mike finally wrapped his arms around her waist and held her tenderly, ignoring his own pain. "Come on...let's sit down. I'll make you some of that herbal tea you like."

She nodded mutely and allowed him to lead her back to the living area. He made certain that she was comfortable before heading into the kitchen to put the yellow kettle on.

It felt like he was having an out-of-body experience as he went into cabinets and took out mugs, tea bags and honey. This couldn't be happening to them...this ugly, mess of a nightmare. She was the love of his life. How could it have come to this?

It was obvious that she was confused and struggling, but so was he. His heart was a twisted knot of misery. Before he could turn the burner on, he found himself sneaking back into the living room to peek and make sure she was still there. He breathed a sigh of relief. She was sitting on the blue toile-print sofa, right where he'd left her.

Their eyes met momentarily and a wealth of unspoken words passed between them. Destiny got up shakily and walked across the room. She just wanted to be near him, to be comforted by her guardian angel. Mike was so warm and strong, his scent so inviting and familiar. It was the most natural thing in the world when they began kissing.

She melted in his arms and suddenly they were in the bedroom and falling backwards onto the plush, yellow, chenille comforter. Mike knew that they should stop, but logic gradually crept out a window and in the end talking was no longer an

132

option…

He put a pillow over his head to escape the bright slivers of sunshine that streamed through pastel-colored vertical blinds. He reached out to pull Destiny closer and realized he was alone. Jumping up, he threw on his pajama pants and began searching the condo. In his heart he already knew that she was gone, but he continued to call her name as if saying it would force her to magically reappear. In the end, he sat down on the sofa and stared dejectedly at a gilt framed Monet reproduction Destiny had called *Jardin a Montgeron* on the living room wall.

She never even drank her herbal tea…

Chapter 34

Terri had a date on Saturday night. On weekends she usually went home to spend time with her family, but that was life *before* the scandal which had rocked her employer's life. Mike was just grateful for the extra help, especially during those first few transitional months. Terri had been a godsend and had practically put her life on hold to help out wherever she could. Recently, he had insisted that she go out and have some fun. Since a nice guy from school had asked her out on a date weeks ago, she finally decided to take him up on the offer.

"How'd the date go?" Mike asked as she closed the door at 11:30 that night.

"Awful," she muttered, throwing her purse on the coffee table.

"What happened? He sounded like a nice guy…"

"We had an argument," she mumbled.

"About *what*? It was your first date!"

"About you."

Mike looked bewildered. "You're kidding. What about me?"

"He said that the reason I was so distracted was because I didn't really want to be with him."

"And what gave him that impression?"

Terri's gaze shifted. "I sort of talked about you and Ulla all night long."

Mike groaned, feeling sorry for her date. "Was that all?"

"No, he said he got the impression I was already attached and when I became available again to look him up."

"You ought to call him back and set the record straight."

"I don't want to set the record straight!" she swallowed hard. "He was right, I *am* already attached."

"Come again?"

"I mean—this job is the most important thing in my life right now. I just don't have time to date, work, and get a college degree."

"Oh," he said awkwardly. "Well, in my opinion, you're way too young to be so attached to your job; you should get out more. I'm going to turn in for the night. I'm sorry things didn't work out with your date."

"Yeah. I think I'll watch a little TV before I go to bed," she said, snatching up the remote.

Mike lay in his bed staring up at the ceiling. Terri wasn't being honest with him. He could smell a liar a mile away and he had a feeling that her job meant more to her than she was letting on. He hoped he was wrong, because the last thing he needed was his daughter's nanny falling for him. Terri was pretty, intelligent and nuts about Ulla, but, it wouldn't be right. He wasn't attracted to her in that way. Sure, Ramirez was constantly encouraging him to start dating again, but nobody was going to force his hand.

He sighed. Destiny still occupied too much space in his heart and there just wasn't room for anybody else.

Terri wiped her runny nose and then curled up beneath her comforter.

Mike really had no idea. She could still see the baffled expression on his face as he'd questioned her.

How could he not know it?

How could he not sense it?

She cared so very much for him and Ulla. They were like a little family now and she was fiercely loyal and protective of them.

As nice as her date was, all night long she'd kept wishing that it was Mike sitting across the dinner table from her, with Ulla in a high chair near by.

What a terrific mess she'd made of things.

Chapter 35

"Why don't you come to Napa with me this weekend?" Todd asked, wrapping his arms possessively around Destiny's waist and nuzzling her neck. "We could go on one of those wine tasting tours…"

She sighed and zoned out.

Life was so much easier with Todd, so uncomplicated. He catered to her, took care of her and shielded her. Destiny enjoyed spending the weekend aboard his yacht in Newport, racing down the coastline in his *911 Carrera*, and late-night dining at the latest celebrity hot spots. The thought of spending a weekend in Napa was appealing. They could go on a tour then spend the rest of the evening in some cozy bed and breakfast eating chocolate-covered strawberries and guzzling bottles of champagne. She was sure that the press would have a field day, but it no longer mattered.

Her marriage was over.

"You've got yourself a date, Mr. Hamilton!" she said with false cheer.

"Great, I know just the place. I'm going to go toss a few things in an overnight bag."

"Don't you have to make reservations?"

For half a minute he stared at her like she was the greenest thing in Hollywood. "I'm Todd Hamilton. I don't have to make a reservation anywhere."

"Do you like kids?" Destiny asked hesitantly.

Todd sipped his chardonnay and smiled faintly at her. "Where is this coming from?" he asked, already suspecting the answer, but wanting to know exactly where her head was at. Parenting wasn't even the last thing on his mind and she needed to know sooner rather than later. Stars were reproducing at an alarming rate all around them, but he had no desire to jump on the band wagon. He sincerely hoped that Destiny planned on leaving her kid in New York with the cop.

"I have one, you know," she continued, acutely aware that

he hadn't answered her question.

"I know. You've been a busy girl. Are you planning to fight for custody, or something?"

"No. This is no place to raise a child. Ulla's much better off with her father."

Inwardly, Todd sighed with relief. He refused to compete with some other man's brat. It guaranteed an ex in the picture as well and Todd wasn't into threesomes.

He was also glad that breeding hadn't destroyed Destiny's body. Fortunately, she didn't have a stretch mark on her and a few weeks of jogging on the beach was guaranteed to tighten up any leftover baby flab. He had warned her years ago that she had to watch her figure and with the outfits she usually wore in her music videos, constant exercise was a necessity not a luxury. The camera could be cruel, but it could also tell the truth.

Todd's favorite thing in the world was an hour-glass figure. He'd been one of the many applauding Hollywood when it finally learned to appreciate Jennifer Lopez's and Salma Hayek's curves. Personally, he'd been appreciating them for years.

At the moment, Destiny's body was a fuller hour glass and Todd had not made any complaints...yet. Still, if she was going to be attending the year's social events as his arm accessory she had to be flawless. After all, he had his reputation to think of.

Chapter 36

Terri and Mike both jumped up when Ulla's crying at three a.m. shattered the quiet. Since Terri's room was closest to the nursery she was the first to arrive on the scene. She picked up her bawling charge and soothed her in gentle tones as Mike looked on bleary eyed.

"I don't know how you do it," he yawned. "And maintain a 3.8 GPA."

"It helps that most of my classes are online, first of all. The rest of it just becomes second nature," she said cheerfully as she changed Ulla's soaked diaper. "Learning what the different cries mean also helps."

"I'll take your word for it. I'm still learning the *give-me-a-bottle-now* cry."

"Why don't you go back to bed? You have to get up in a few hours. I'm going to give the princess here a bottle and then she's going back in the crib."

Ulla chortled and tugged on Terri's long ponytail, as if to say she had other plans.

Mike kissed one of his daughter's chubby hands and was rewarded with delighted babbling. "Sleep tight, baby. Daddy will see you in a few hours." He looked gratefully at Terri. "By the way, before I forget again," Mike said pausing with his hand on the doorframe.

"Yeah?"

"We're going to be moving and I'd hate to have to change up nannies on Ulla with everything that's happened. Would you be willing to commute to Long Island?"

"No need to even ask. I'll see you in the morning, Mike."

"Thanks, Terri. You're a lifesaver."

"And you are welcome," she said with a warm smile. "Now, go!"

"You don't have to tell me twice. Good night."

"Buenos noches," Terri said softly, watching him leave. She sighed unconsciously. She was in this thing for the long haul.

Maybe one day Mike would get a revelation.

Chapter 37

"Hi, gorgeous," Todd said with his trademark grin.

"Hi, yourself," Destiny replied, not even sparing him a second glance, as she abandoned The History Channel in favor of the Home Shopping Network. Since Todd was grinning from ear to ear she had to assume that they had been invited to another extravagant Hollywood bash where they would play the happy IT couple role and make all the right contacts.

She was sick of it. How many connections did a person need to make in Hollywood anyway? How many favors? When was enough *enough*?

"I've got a surprise for you," Todd said, taking the remote out of her hand and ignoring the peeved expression on her face. "I promise you'll like it," he said in the husky voice that used to really get her going.

"Okay, Todd. I give up. What is it? Another party in the Hills?"

He dangled a set of car keys in front of her face. "Not even close."

"What are those for?"

"*Those* are the keys to your new ride," he announced with a sexy grin. "Take a look outside."

What in the world had he done? Destiny's legs suddenly felt weak. She raced over to the window and looked down into the driveway. Parked next to Todd's blue Porsche 911 Turbo was a metallic red Corvette Z06 with a seriously large white bow on its hood.

"Happy birthday, baby," Todd whispered in her ear, as he pressed the keys into her trembling hand.

"Todd, you remembered," she breathed, her eyes glistening. Destiny threw her arms around his neck and kissed him. "You didn't have to do this."

"I know, but I wanted to. Besides, I remember what you told me years ago—"

"That one day when I became rich and famous I was going

to buy one."

"It's even better when somebody just *gives* you one, isn't it?"

"I've got to take her for a spin!" she blurted excitedly, wiping her eyes.

"It's your birthday, gorgeous—"

"Hold that thought," she said planting another kiss on him. "I'm going to change into something more comfortable."

Todd winked at her as she dashed out of the living room and down the hallway to her walk-in closet that was practically a room itself. "Checkmate," he murmured with a satisfied smile.

Forty-five minutes later Destiny sauntered back into the living room. "Ready for that ride?" she purred.

Todd saw her in the plate glass window before he turned around. He had a hunch that D&G had designed the satin, corset dress; but even they could not have anticipated how outrageously hot his woman was going to look in it.

Destiny was beyond ready for her close-up. From her makeup to her red stiletto sandals sparkling with Swarovski crystals she was dressing the part of the big screen siren and Todd was loving it. He made a mental note to text his favorite journalist. All of this was definitely not going to be wasted driving around the coastline in the dark. It was time for another night out on the town.

"Like I've said before, gorgeous, red is definitely your color."

Chapter 38

"Hey, princess," Mike whispered, as he scooped Ulla out of the big reclining chair in the den and kissed the top of her head of unruly chocolate curls. She murmured incoherently and wrapped her arms tightly around her father's neck.

"Ready to go sleepy?" he asked. The child's head fell lazily against his shoulder. "I'll take that as a yes."

Mike carried Ulla down the hallway to her Blues Clues decorated bedroom, placed her in the center of her toddler bed and tucked her in tightly.

These moments were precious to him. At the end of a stress-filled day on the job this was what he loved coming home to...his baby. She made everything worthwhile.

He would never be able to understand how her mother could so easily abandon her. Especially since Ulla was a miniature version of Destiny. True, Ulla had Mike's dimples and coloring, but everything else came from her mother, the mother who had skipped off to Hollywood and broken his heart. Even now his arms ached to hold Destiny.

Mike clutched the headboard on Ulla's bed and shut his eyes. It shouldn't be possible to still love and miss someone so much. There was a constant ache in the pit of his belly that he couldn't seem to get rid of and the thought of trusting anyone again seemed impossible. He even struggled with trusting God. After all, God was not supposed to allow Mike to be tempted beyond what he could handle...He must have known that Destiny was going to be too much.

Let her go. She's a broad path of pain and destruction for you.

God's words suddenly came back to haunt Mike. Why hadn't he listened? Why did he allow the devil to take him on that ride?

...men who were brought low by a pretty face.

Now his pastor's words were echoing through his mind.

This was beyond low and the pain and humiliation were

indescribable.

Mike knelt in front of his daughter's bed and held his head in his hands. Because of his disobedience Ulla was now living in a broken home and might never experience God's plan for a healthy family relationship and he had no one to blame but himself. Mike had allowed his lust to dictate his actions and now he was paying the price. The only thing that he did not regret—would never regret—was the result of his sin. Because of his baby girl, Mike knew he was still capable of love and that there was hope for a brighter future.

Terri was walking past Ulla's room to get herself a late-night glass of water from the kitchen when she heard the unmistakable sound of sobbing. Heart racing, she leaned silently against the wall in the dimly-lit hallway. She knew why he was crying…this wasn't the first time she had heard him.

Mike was still mourning the loss of his marriage. Some days it seemed as though he would never recover, other days he appeared fine.

Terri wanted desperately to rush into that room like a cavalry and rescue Mike from himself. She wanted to absorb all of his pain and fill him with all of the love that she had for him; she wanted him to take from her whatever he needed to heal. But it would probably just embarrass him if she were to intrude. Frustrated, she crept back down the hallway to the guest room and carefully shut the door. She burrowed beneath the soft, warm comforter and cried herself to sleep.

Chapter 39

"Wow, she gets prettier every year, doesn't she?" Destiny reflected.

Todd sauntered over to see what she was referring to, although he already had a hunch. There was a photograph of her now four-year-old daughter on some beach with her nanny. She was a pretty kid—there was no denying it. The press was going to enjoy taking pictures of her for a very long time.

Nothing like being born into stardom, he thought sarcastically.

Destiny's fascination with her former family had to end, though. She had a scrapbook filled with tabloid photos of her kid…and the cop. She kept it hidden in the bottom of an armoire, but Todd already knew about it. He was going to toss the thing one day while she was out.

Maybe he needed to get her pregnant. A new baby might help her to get her focus back on their relationship. The media would certainly love it.

He decided to go for the kill while she was feeling nostalgic.

"How'd you like another one of those?" he asked, massaging her shoulders.

"You don't even like children," she replied, reaching for a pair of scissors so that she could cut out the latest acquisition for her scrapbook.

"You could change my mind."

"Don't play with me, Todd."

He tilted her chin upwards and gazed directly into her eyes. "I'm not playing. We could start working on one tonight."

"I'm on the Pill, remember? It's not that simple," she said moodily. "Besides, I'm a lousy mother and you'd make a terrible father. I wouldn't wish us on a stranger's baby, much less our own."

"Ouch! The next time I need someone to bring me down a couple of notches remind me to hire you."

She sighed and looked up at him with melancholy eyes. "I'm sorry. I don't know what's going on with me today."

Destiny's heart was heavy.

Why were all of these feelings surfacing now? Was it the tabloid photo she'd recently seen of Terri and Ulla out shopping, or the one of Terri, Ulla and Mike hanging out by the infamous Bethesda Fountain in New York?

That was Destiny's family. Those were supposed to be *her* experiences! And now the media was hinting at a possible budding romance between Mike and Terri...a prospect that did not sit well with Destiny. She wanted Mike to be happy, but not with the hired help! The mere thought irritated her. How annoyingly cliché!

Destiny knew that she was being selfish. The ink had dried on their divorce papers years ago. If anyone deserved a shot at happiness it was Mike. God knew she had put him through enough hell. Besides, Terri had been a better mother to Ulla than she had ever been. Destiny wondered if her child even knew who she was and for some reason the thought hurt. Part of her wanted to pick up the phone, dial Mike's home number and just listen to her little girl speak. Part of her wanted to scratch the nanny's eyes out. It was amazing how territorial she'd become over something she no longer had a right to.

Collecting photos and articles about her former family couldn't be a good thing either. How could she ever let go of the past if it was constantly staring her in the face?

Destiny slammed the scrapbook shut and ignored the sob that had been rising in her throat all afternoon.

Chapter 40

"Destiny?" Mike said hesitantly when she finally answered her cell phone a few days later.

"Mike?" she groggily replied. "What time is it?"

"It's late. Listen, I don't want you to be alarmed—"

She immediately sat up in the bed. "What's going on?"

"It's Ulla. She's in the hospital with pneumonia."

"What?! How?"

"She's a kid, Destiny. It happens sometimes. Anyway, she's in the children's unit at Long Island Jewish and her pediatrician's optimistic. It's not necessary for you to fly out here."

"Then, why'd you call me?" she asked.

"It's the right thing to do. Besides, she was asking for you when the fever hit."

"I'll be there first thing tomorrow," Destiny said, jumping up from the bed and heading to her closet.

"You don't have to," Mike reiterated.

"She's still my daughter, too. Thanks for the call. I'll see you in a few hours."

"Is it really necessary for you to leave right now?" Todd asked with an annoyed expression. "You know how tight the schedule is."

Destiny stopped packing for a moment to glare at him. She wasn't even going to ask him where he'd been last night when she'd received the disturbing news; at the moment it just wasn't important. "We're talking about *my child*, Todd. I'll be back before your next appointment at the spa, so relax. The director's going to shoot around me for the next couple of days."

"Are you sure it's just your daughter that's got you running back to New York?" he said with a raised brow.

"Now who's being paranoid?" she asked defensively, zipping up a carry-on bag. "My driver's already waiting outside, I'll call you as soon as I land." She gave him a kiss and hurried to the front door. "Try to behave while I'm away," she half teased.

Todd snorted rudely and picked up his cell phone the moment she was gone. "Hey, Matt, you up for a little club action tonight? Invite the Brazilian twins while you're at it…"

***

Ulla had only been a few months old the last time Destiny had seen her. She didn't expect the child to remember her. So she'd been stunned to hear that Ulla had asked for her. How could she *not* go?

The flight was a blur. The private jet arrived at MacArthur airport in record time and a car was already awaiting her arrival. Destiny didn't even wait for the driver to open the door when they arrived at the hospital; she jumped out of the back seat and raced inside the building…

Destiny donned a disposable face mask and thoroughly washed her hands before entering Ulla's room. She was pleased to hear nothing but good reports from the pediatric staff about her daughter's condition. Tiptoeing into the private room, Destiny paused at the foot of her child's bed, astonished by a sudden wave of emotion. This was what she had expected to feel the day Ulla was first placed in her arms. Now she understood why Mike had fought so hard against her wish to abort. Their daughter epitomized everything that had been good, pure, and beautiful about their marriage. For the very first time, she felt genuinely ashamed and selfish about how she had treated her little girl. Destiny carefully hung her coat and handbag on a door hook, gently stroked the sleeping child's forehead and then curled up in a chair beside Ulla's bed and fell asleep.

Mike found himself whistling as he walked down the corridor to Ulla's room, an oversized *Blues Clues* plush tucked under one arm. He threw on the brakes when he arrived and peeked inside the open door. Destiny and Ulla were in bed, watching cartoons and laughing. For a moment Mike battled a surge of anger and resentment. This is what it took for her to come home and be a decent mother? He was about to walk away and come back later, when Destiny's eyes suddenly met his.

"Mike! Wait…please!" Destiny gave Ulla a quick kiss on

the cheek and then scrambled off the bed. "Mommy will be right back, okay?"

The little girl nodded slowly, her aqua-colored eyes uncertain. "Where'd daddy go?"

"That's what mommy's going to find out. I promise I'll be right back."

Mike was already halfway down the corridor and headed in the direction of the elevator bank by the time she caught up to him.

"I've got a few errands to run," he replied with a cool glance. "I can come back later this evening."

"No. I'll leave," she said softly, fighting to keep her hands to herself. He was overdue for a haircut. Mike never allowed it to grow out because it became too unruly and uncomfortable under his police hat. She thought his hair looked fantastic, but knew it was a losing battle to ask him to leave it alone. "Ulla's doing great," she said lamely, some part of her willing him to stay. "The doctor said that she'll be able to go home by tomorrow."

Mike remained silent. He already knew that. Some perverse part of him was determined to make his ex as uncomfortable as possible. She had really come. He still couldn't believe it. She had actually honored her word for a change!

Her acting ability had also improved, because he'd swear that he had never seen a more sincere expression on any mother's face.

"I can leave now if you'd like to go in and see her," Destiny suggested, noticing the stuffed blue toy under his arm.

"Would you?" Mike asked caustically and then wished he could retract those words. The wounded look he saw in her eyes was definitely not rehearsed. Jesus would not have handled things that way; Mike was immediately convicted in his spirit. "I'm sorry. That was uncalled for."

Destiny held up her hand to stop him. "Don't. I deserved that. I'll tell Ulla that I'll be back tomorrow."

Mike nodded his head and resisted watching his ex-wife walk back down the corridor. Even dressed down she exuded stardom...

148

He must have been out of his mind to ever get involved with her.

***

Destiny was surprised to see Mike standing outside the door of her condo after the icy reception she had received from him at the hospital. Still, she'd instructed security to allow him upstairs, no questions asked.

"Would you like something to drink?" she asked politely, fidgeting with freshly wrapped nails behind her back.

"No. Look, I can't do this!" Mike abruptly exclaimed, catching her off guard.

"Do what?"

"Pretend that seeing you isn't upsetting me! Pretend that I don't care about what you've done with your life for the past four years! Pretend that I've gone on with my own life and that I never think about you! God knows that I've tried to move on, that I've tried to get over you—"

Stunned, Destiny wrapped her arms around her waist to keep from shaking.

He still loved her!

Part of her wanted to shout with joy, the other part wasn't sure how to respond.

"It's okay," she whispered tentatively.

He opened his eyes.

"I still—"

"Don't," he warned. "Don't say anything….please…just don't."

"Then why did you come here?" she frowned, barely able to breathe from the onslaught of emotions threatening to consume them both.

"I couldn't stay away. I want so much to touch you, hold you and kiss you. I want to make love to you until you forget any other man that's ever put his hands on you. But most of all, I want to stop hurting every time I see or think or hear about you."

Mike had always had a way with words, but that night, for some reason, they were overwhelming to her. Destiny suddenly felt lightheaded, began to sway and would have collapsed if he hadn't rushed to catch her.

Resting her head against his strong shoulder, she slowly exhaled. She hadn't felt this safe in a long time. She knew that she could trust Mike Reilly with her life.

He sat down on the sofa and held her until the room stopped spinning.

"Are you okay?" he said with concern. "I'm sorry—I shouldn't have come."

"Yes, you should've. I wanted to see you, but was too afraid to call."

"But you weren't too afraid to come to the hospital?" he noted.

Destiny sighed. "I knew you'd be there."

Mike looked as though he was about to say something and then changed his mind. He slowly stood up. "It's late. I'd better be going."

She scrambled off the sofa and stood in front of him. "Don't leave…"

"I know how much you hate it," he whispered, cupping her chin with one hand. "But if I don't go now—"

"Kiss me first," she pleaded. "It's one of the things I've missed the most."

Mike gazed at her for a long time, reacquainting himself with her exotic features, the shape of her eyes, the curve of her lips and then he kissed her so thoroughly that it left her gasping for air.

"Do you want me to pick you up tomorrow?" he finally murmured.

"Yes," she breathed raggedly.

"Try and get some sleep," he suggested, as he headed for the door.

The next day when Mike arrived at Destiny's building, the first thing he noticed was that she looked tired and sad. Then he noticed some suitcases by the door.

"What's going on?" he asked, confused. Last night had meant something to him. He thought it had been the same for her.

"I'm sorry, Mike. I'm not going to be able to go. My agent called this morning. I'm in the middle of filming a movie and the schedule is tight. They can't spare me another 24 hours—"

"So, what am I supposed to tell our daughter?" he asked, trying to keep his tone neutral. "That making a movie is more important to her mother than spending time with her?"

Destiny chewed her bottom lip and looked away. She felt so torn. Couldn't he see that? More than anything she wanted to pick up where they had left off the previous night, as well as spend more time with their daughter. Why couldn't he cut her some slack?

"There's a limo waiting downstairs for me. I have to leave. Please explain to Ulla for me. I don't want to go to the hospital and upset her."

"Fine…go do what you have to do, Destiny. I'll pick up the pieces, as usual."

"Mike, wait, about last night—"

"Forget it ever happened. Take care of yourself," he said, as he headed towards the elevator.

Destiny's eyes filled with tears. She had a sinking feeling that she had just missed the boat. Again.

***

"What the hell is this?" Todd asked, practically shoving a newspaper under Destiny's nose as soon as she walked into the house in Malibu.

She glanced at the photo and groaned internally. Someone had taken a picture of Mike leaving her condo in New York at a really suspicious time of morning. The caption read: *Destiny and 'New York's Finest'…On Again?*

She slapped the paper away. "Nothing happened, Todd. He just came by to talk."

"One journalist said that he didn't leave until nearly sunrise! What was so important that it couldn't wait?"

"Our daughter's health?" Destiny said with an arched brow.

"Bull! You do know that people at the studio have probably seen this—"

"So that's what this is all about!" she exploded, glaring at him. "You don't care about what I was doing alone with my ex—all you care about is the stupid movie!"

Todd visibly calmed himself, although his tone remained icy. "I do care. No more jaunts to the Big Apple for you, gorgeous. From now on, it's all work and no play. If the cop needs to discuss something about your kid tell him to pick up the phone."

"You can't tell me what to do with my life *or* my child!" she hissed, looking at him as though he had lost his mind.

"You're right. However, if word gets around town that you're an unreliable diva and that investors' dollars are being squandered trying to film around you so that you can run off to the East Coast to play house with some cop—let's just see how long you last in this business."

Destiny watched speechless as he stormed out of the room.

He had just threatened her career.

Chapter 41

"Why are you doing this to yourself?" Terri asked, as Mike flipped over the newspaper article about him and Destiny.

"Because I still love her—" he said with a half-hearted shrug. "Why does anyone allow another human being to treat them poorly?"

"I wish that I hadn't gone away on vacation that week. Why didn't you call me?" Terri hated the fact that he had reached out to his unsupportive ex on the West Coast. Even if she was Ulla's mother.

"You had relatives fly in from another country for that reunion. I wasn't going to tear you away from your family when I had everything under control here. When are you going to stop taking all of this so personally?"

A faint blush stained her cheeks before she found her voice. "I just hate seeing you and Ulla get hurt over and over again."

"We'll be okay," Mike consoled himself. "I just have to remind my heart that the marriage is over. Destiny's obviously got better things to do."

"Well, I think she's crazy! That actor she's with is such an arrogant, self-centered—it's just a wonder that he has time for anyone other than himself!"

"I'll take it you're not his biggest fan," Mike said with a chuckle, as Terri tore into a KFC drumstick.

"Never was. I've got a thing about people who are in love with themselves."

"So how long have you disliked my former wife?" he asked with a knowing look.

Terri put the fried chicken down and glanced sheepishly at him. "For years. I mean, way before I ever started working for you guys."

"Why?"

"Truthfully? I'm not fond of most of the people in the entertainment industry. They all seem a bit too superficial and high maintenance to me. Although after getting to know Destiny a little I have to admit that she's a bit more down to earth than most. Can I ask you a personal question?"

"Sure."

"What made you fall for her—I mean—besides the obvious?" she asked making an imaginary hour glass shape in the air with her hands.

"Believe it or not, there's a side of her that only those really close to her know about," he reflected, his eyes softening.

"The media made a big deal out of your meeting back at her place," Terri said, abruptly changing the subject.

"They're always going to make a big deal about anything Destiny does, but, I've got a feeling that you especially were not happy to hear that bit of news," pinning her with that gem-like stare.

"No, I wasn't," she said, staring aimlessly at the half-eaten drumstick. "I just had a feeling you'd end up getting hurt again."

"In her defense, she wanted to stay, but the powers that be were barking for her to come back to Hollywood."

"If you and Ulla were mine it wouldn't have been an issue—that studio would've had to find themselves a new actress!"

Mike didn't know what to say. A part of him felt the same way. The other part understood that there might have been legal ramifications if Destiny had not complied.

"How could she value the two of you so little? Why is her family always last on her list of priorities—"

He suddenly slammed his hands down on the kitchen table causing Terri to jump. "Not another word! My personal life is no longer open for discussion and if that's a problem for you—" He didn't bother to wait for her to respond. She had unknowingly struck a painful nerve and Mike had to get out of there before he said something he'd later regret. Shoving his chair back, he stormed out of the kitchen.

A few hours later Mike heard Terri moving around in the kitchen. He listened to the refrigerator door open and close, heard her pop open a soda can. He was embarrassed for getting bent out of shape and wanted to apologize. It wasn't her fault that she was decent and loyal and that he just wasn't used to it.

"Hi," he said softly, leaning against the doorway.

She looked up at him and he immediately felt like a heel; there was such a wounded expression in her eyes. "Hi."

"Hey, I'm sorry for earlier…there's no excuse."

"No need to apologize. I overstepped. My oldest sister always tells me that I never know when to shut up."

"Well if you don't accept my apology—"

"Apology accepted," she said with a wry smile.

"Whatcha got there?"

"A root beer float in progress. You interested?"

"Absolutely," he said, pulling up a chair.

Terri filled two metal tumblers with soda, put generous scoops of French vanilla ice cream in both, sprayed some whipped cream and garnished with cherries. Then she put long-handled spoons in each and handed one to Mike.

He took a sip and grinned with satisfaction. "Now *that's* how it's supposed to be done! Thanks, Terri, you're the best!"

She watched as he left the kitchen to go check out his favorite action series in the den. Hoping he'd invite her to join him was futile…obviously she was only "the best" for some things.

Chapter 42

"You know, that Terri's a sweetheart. You should bring her," Ramirez stated nonchalantly. It was his brother's anniversary party that evening and he'd been hounding Mike for weeks about going.

"And who'll watch Ulla?" Mike asked, trying not to give his friend a look. He knew what Dave was up to and he wasn't interested.

"Bring her, too! I've got a few nieces and nephews she can play with. C'mon, Reilly! It'll be fun and besides, you need to get out and get some fresh air, my friend."

Mike kept his gaze trained on the Jason Statham action flick he was watching.

Ramirez sighed. It was fast approaching year five of his divorce and Mike was still in a funk. He hated to tell his partner that he'd told him so, but Mike needed to wake up and smell the espresso! How many of those celebrity marriages actually lasted? It took more than good looks to make a marriage work. Mike deserved a woman whose first priority was her family, not a career. If only Reilly had listened to him!

"So, you going or not?" Ramirez pressed.

Mike threw his hands up. "You're like a dog with a bone—did you know that?"

"And I won't quit until you give me an answer."

"Fine, Ramirez! I'll go, alright?"

"How about I set you up with somebody?" his partner asked helpfully.

"I don't think so. I said I'd go. Don't push your luck!"

***

Terri looked at her cell phone. Mike was sending her an urgent text message:

Sorry for the short notice, but I have to go to an anniversary party tonight and if I show up alone Ramirez is going to try to hook me up with one of his crazy cousins. Please say that you can go. I'm BEGGING! My parents will watch

156

Ulla. Let me know. Thanks!

Panicked, Terri rushed over to her older sister's house for help after she accepted Mike's invitation to the party. It was just like a man to ask a woman out on such short notice to such a special event. She didn't have anything decent in her closet and no time to go shopping. Fortunately, her sister was a buyer for a major department store and enjoyed the occasional makeover.

"Look at me, Maritza," Terri groaned. "How could I ever compete with someone like his ex? I don't even know what to wear!"

Maritza stared at her sister for a second, then opened the door of her closet and pulled out a black haltered evening gown that could at the very least cause a fender bender. "It's not about competing, little sis'. It's about working with what you've already got," she said holding the dress up in front of Terri. "You're so busy being hard on yourself that you can't see what the rest of us do. That gorgeous hair, those lashes that only Maybelline can create for most of us, that flawless skin—come on," Maritza said, taking her by the hand.

"Where are we going?"

"We're going to get you ready for that party tonight. Just think of me as your fairy godmother!"

***

"Whoa! Look at you!" Mike exclaimed, when he picked Terri up from her sister's house later that evening. She looked incredible. He rushed to open the door on the passenger side of his vehicle for her and waited for her to buckle up before he closed it. Their eyes met momentarily. Terri blushed and Mike grinned like a teenager. It had been awhile since he'd been out on a date with a pretty woman and suddenly he was looking forward to it.

"Mike?" Teresa said with a little smile, waving a hand in front of him to get his attention.

An unnecessary gesture, because she already had it. That was why he was so distracted. Mike had never seen Teresa fully made up, fresh from the hair salon and wearing a killer dress like the one she had on.

How was it possible that the woman had been living under his roof for the past few years and he had never noticed what a knockout she was?

Teresa flipped 40's movie star waves over one ivory shoulder and then crossed her legs. Mike's mouth went dry.

Whoa! What was going on here? He had never thought of himself as easily seducible, but ever since Destiny had turned his world upside down he was no longer certain. He was drooling over his daughter's nanny, for crying out loud!

"Hey, are you alright?" Teresa asked, concern marring her perfectly sculpted brows.

"Yeah...I'm good. It's just a little warm in here."

"Want to get some fresh air? I've got a feeling they won't be cutting the cake for a while."

"Sure, why not?" he replied, trying not to stare as she stood up. It was amazing what people could conceal beneath oversized, everyday garments.

Mike unconsciously placed his hand on the small of her back and Teresa resisted the urge to shiver with delight. It had taken awhile to get to this point with him, but she really felt as though their relationship had finally turned a corner. *She was actually out on a real date with Mike Reilly!* How often had she dreamt about this moment?

She smiled generously at a couple of young women casting envious glances her way. Teresa felt their pain—or at least she had once upon a time. Now it was open season and Teresa planned on taking home the prize!

Internally she said a prayer of thanks for her older sister. The woman truly was a fairy godmother. If the way Mike had ogled her at their table was any indication about her appearance, then Maritza deserved a month of free baby sitting services!

The catering facility was a romantic's dream come true. There were partially concealed alcoves with chaise lounges sprinkled throughout, balconies with French doors, a garden

158

maze tastefully decorated with beautiful stone fountains of Greek statuettes and wrought iron bistro furnishings.

Teresa was delighted to discover a swinging loveseat partially hidden by an enormous wisteria tree near a small pond. She squealed with delight and grabbed Mike's hand.

"I'll race you!" she blurted.

"In *that* dress?" he asked incredulously.

Teresa kicked off her high heels with a grin. "Watch me!"

"Hey!" Mike yelled, as she hiked up her gown and left him in the dust. She was actually pretty fast, but he managed to outrun her and jumped in front of the swing before she could.

Laughing, while attempting to catch her breath, Teresa waved an imaginary white flag. "You win!"

"Thanks for admitting your defeat," Mike said with a smile, offering her a seat on the swing.

"Thanks for not rubbing it in," she graciously replied, as she sat beside him.

They relaxed in companionable silence for awhile, simply enjoying the fresh air, lush landscape and brilliant sunset. When Terri finally dared to glance at Mike she felt her heart skip a beat. He looked so handsome in his black tuxedo with aquamarine cuff links which complimented his eyes. She still couldn't believe that they were out together.

"Thanks again for inviting me, Mike," she said sincerely.

"Thanks again for accepting. This has actually been fun."

"We do need to work on your salsa technique, but other than that—"

"My Latin ballroom moves are a little rusty," he said with a sheepish grin.

"It's okay. I saw at least ten ladies who were willing to come to your rescue!"

Mike laughed. He really was enjoying himself. He couldn't remember the last time he'd had such a great time and it put his mind at ease knowing that Ulla was with his parents until Sunday evening. He was glad that they still had enough energy left in them to keep up with their granddaughter. She was a handful, but she was the apple of their eye.

***

A blaring television commercial woke Mike up. Disoriented, he sat in the dark for a few minutes, the only illumination coming from the streetlights outside. He moved to get up from the sofa and realized that he wasn't alone. Terri was sleeping in the crook of his arm, her legs tucked beneath her, one arm draped over his midsection. They must have dozed off after watching a re-run of his favorite sitcom. He gave her shoulder a little shake and her head lolled sideways. Then she murmured his name...so softly it was almost a sigh. Mike gazed down at her. This woman loved him and his child unconditionally. She didn't have to say it. Her every action spoke volumes. She was everything a man could desire in a mate.

If only he had met her first.

He moved a dark silken strand away from her face. She'd looked awesome that night in the black halter dress and more than a couple of guys had cast an admiring glance her way. Mike was proud to have her on his arm.

Terri's eyes fluttered open and the first thing she noticed was Mike staring at her, as though really seeing her for the very first time and then he kissed her. It was the type of kiss one saw in movies, the type that made toes curl and could make a weak woman give in when she should stand her ground and resist.

If there had been any doubts in her mind about her feelings for Mike they were laid to rest in that moment, which was why she felt confused when he abruptly released her. She gazed up at him questioningly, wondering if she'd done something wrong.

"I'm sorry," Mike began. "I shouldn't have done that."

"Done what? What are you apologizing for?" she said with a puzzled look.

"You looked so gorgeous tonight," he rambled. He prided himself on being a gentleman and his behavior was inappropriate. Terri wasn't the type of girl you had your way with on a sofa! She was a nice girl, a good friend, and Ulla's nanny.

What was he thinking?!

"This was a mistake," he announced.

"Which part, Mike? Taking me out on a date? Kissing

160

me? Or finally realizing that it's okay to open your heart again after somebody you love tap dances all over it?"

"Terri, I respect you and I care about you. I don't want you to get hurt."

"You know something, Mike? Next time, don't do me any favors!" She fled down the hallway to her room, where she had the pleasure of slamming the door so hard the frame shook.

Fifteen minutes later Mike was knocking softly.

"Go away! This is definitely not the time," she sniffled, grateful that she had already washed off her makeup and mascara.

"Let me in, Terri. We need to talk," he said patiently.

"Not interested."

"I can stand here all night."

"It's your house—be my guest!"

"Wow and all this time I thought that you were such a nice, quiet, Latina—"

The door suddenly swung open. "I *am* a nice Latina. But there's nothing quiet about me. If you'd open your eyes and ears for five minutes you'd know that! Look, I thought when you asked me out that you were ready to move on. Obviously you were just looking for a buddy, not an actual date. That was *my* mistake. It won't happen again."

"You deserve more than a quickie on a sofa…and much more than a cop who's still picking up the pieces," Mike said softly, amused by the way her accent had thickened.

Terri felt the steam leave her. Who could stay angry with this man for any amount of time? She felt her heart cave in. "I'd like to help you pick up those pieces."

"You shouldn't have to. You're just an innocent bystander."

"I stopped being an *innocent bystander* the moment my heart got involved."

"You were crying," he stated, noticing a streak on her face.

She shook her head. "Yeah…must be hormones or something. No big deal."

"Liar," Mike said, gently wiping the streak away with his thumb.

"Don't," she rasped, capturing his hand.

"Why not?"

"Because it hurts too much when you touch me. Good night, Mike."

Mike was lying in bed and staring up at the ceiling. It had been an evening full of revelations. He cared about Terri and her feelings...way more than an employer or friend should. And it was scary.

He was still in love with Destiny. *Wasn't he?*

God help him.

Everything had suddenly become much more complicated.

***

The following day was bizarre for both of them and it seemed the meal at the breakfast table couldn't end quickly enough.

"I'm moving back into my sister's house," Terri blurted. "I think it's best."

"You're making a really big deal over nothing," Mike said flipping through the sports section of a newspaper.

Terri yanked the paper down so that he was forced to look at her. "We can't go on like this. Last night changed everything for me! I can't pretend nothing happened... even if you can and I don't feel comfortable living here any more."

"Would you be feeling comfortable if we'd made love?"

Terri almost knocked over her coffee cup. He could be a real straight shooter when he wanted to be. She did want to make love with him....preferably as his wife. There was no other man on Earth that she'd rather surrender her innocence to. "I can't do this," she finally said. "I'm tired of pretending that it's okay for everything to remain status quo."

Mike didn't know what to say. He no longer viewed her as just an employee in his home; she had become much more and they both knew it.

"I'll stop by later to pick up my things."

"Terri, wait," he said, standing up so quickly his chair fell over.

"I can't, Mike. I've waited long enough!" she turned on

her heel and was about to flee the kitchen, when he grabbed her hand and gently pulled her back to him.

She was sobbing as he hugged her tightly. He cared deeply about Terri, but part of him was afraid to trust and love again.

The doorbell suddenly rang.

"It's probably Ramirez," he said softly. "He said he'd be stopping by today."

"Go answer it then," Terri smiled tremulously. "We don't want him kicking down the front door to save his partner."

"We'll finish talking later," Mike promised as he ran to open the door.

"No we won't," she whispered sadly.

"Is it me, or is it hot in here?" Ramirez asked with a smirk.

"It's always you. How's it going, man?" Mike said hugging his friend.

"It's going. A few of my cousins were checking you out last night. Did you see anyone you liked? I'll hook it up."

"Why is it always about women with you?"

"What else is there? We're both young, single and have the privilege of wearing a uniform that's a bigger chick magnet than military dress whites, my friend!"

"There's more to life, Ramirez."

"Whatever. You looked like you were having a good time with the nanny—man, does she clean up nice!"

"The nanny's got a name," Mike said deadpan.

"Okay, okay! Don't bite my head off! Did you have a nice evening with *Teresa*?" Ramirez asked over-enunciating her name.

"Affirmative."

Ramirez whooped for joy until Mike gave him another look. "Is she here?"

"Yeah, so please use your inside voice."

"She's a good egg, that one. You should make sure you don't let her get away."

Mike didn't reply. He was already letting her get away and he hoped that he didn't live to regret it.

Chapter 43

Destiny looked around the dressing room in a panic and then paused when she caught sight of her anxious reflection in the mirror. The Roberto Cavalli gown was stunning, the Harry Winston diamonds impeccable and every platinum-streaked tendril had been coaxed into an elegant French roll…she couldn't figure out what was wrong, or why she'd been seized by a sadness so profound it brought tears to her eyes. She sat down dejectedly, vaguely aware of the splendid array of flowers on either side of the vanity, compliments of the theater and her agent.

Opening a drawer, she pulled out an old photograph of her family which she had recently started taking with her everywhere. It was from a layout done by *In Style* magazine. Mike was wearing flax-colored linen pants and cradling two-month old Ulla against his bare chest. It was a fantastic shot and the expression on Mike's face—the joy and love radiating from him—was an almost tangible thing. It made Destiny want to leap into the picture just to bask in its glow. She held the photo up and then brought it to her lips. "I love you," she whispered, putting it back into the drawer.

Standing up, she gave herself a mental shake, smoothed the beading on her gown and walked towards the door. She wasn't up to performing a single note that evening, but she had promised to do the VH1 Diva special and after all was said and done the show still had to go on…

Going home in her limo, Destiny held her head in her hands and wept bitterly. She had everything she'd ever dreamt of and it didn't mean a thing.

She missed Mike; missed his gentle touch, warm smile and tender heart. She must have been out of her mind to get involved with Todd again. That man was so shallow he could make a puddle look deep. And her new personal assistant was a joke. Half the time the girl was so star struck she bordered on useless. Destiny wondered absently what Chelsea was up to. She missed her old assistant. But then, she was missing a lot of things lately…thank God Bill was still on the payroll!

Destiny felt the limo fishtail. The driver had sped up when a couple of vehicles carrying crazed fans decided they had to have a few more pictures of the movie star. Then everything happened really fast—not in slow motion the way it sometimes does in the movies when something bad is about to occur. Destiny didn't have time to blink, or watch her life flash before her eyes. An SUV got too close and sideswiped the limo, causing it to swerve out of control and careen toward an overpass. The metallic taste of fear filled Destiny's mouth as a scream emerged and metal and cement collided violently.

Then everything went black.

She awoke to the sounds of police sirens and someone calling her name. Miraculously, she and her driver were uninjured. But she could see that the other vehicle that had struck them was upside down with a crushed hood. Gasoline and glass now littered the highway.

A police officer was tugging on the damaged door, his partner a few feet away speaking rapidly into a mic on the shoulder of his uniform. The officer quickly unbuckled her seat belt and scooped her up in his arms. "The ambulance will be here any second, ma'am. Are you in any pain?"

Destiny slowly shook her head as he carried her away from the wreckage.

"You don't seem to have a scratch on you. Somebody must be praying for you somewhere."

She glanced back at the limo and began trembling uncontrollably. It was a mangled mess of glass and steel and a couple of the tires had been knocked off. Destiny couldn't believe that she wasn't being carried out in a body bag; even her driver had only suffered a bump on his head. As an EMT put an oxygen mask over her face and began checking her vitals the words of the police officer returned to her.

Somebody must be praying for you somewhere.

It was all over the news the following morning, even

though Destiny had already been released from the hospital. Mike jumped out of bed when he saw it on the news. He snatched a suitcase out of his closet and began to mindlessly throw items into it.

Don't go to her.

Mike stopped what he was doing and just stood in the middle of the room. It had been a long time since God had said anything to him concerning Destiny. "But that's my wife!"

That was your wife. Remember: those who are willing and obedient are the ones who eat the good of the land.

Mike sat back down on his bed, stunned. If God was telling him not to go, there had to be a good reason. He wouldn't be disobedient this time…even if it was breaking his heart and he was five minutes away from screaming with aggravation. He immediately dropped to his knees and began to pray for the strength to accept God's command.

Chapter 44

Two months after the car accident that could have claimed her life, Destiny found herself preparing to go to yet another movie premiere with Todd. She suddenly stopped slipping on her favorite Jimmy Choos to glance at him. He'd been overwrought, concerned, and solicitous at the hospital when he'd come to pick her up, but as soon as the reporters and their camera crews were out of sight...

"Do you love me?" Destiny asked pointedly, her bottom lip starting to quiver. She'd never heard him say those words to her and suddenly it was as though her life depended on it. She had to hear him say it.

Todd stopped adjusting his silk tie in the mirror and stared at her reflection for a second. "We're going to be late. Let's talk about this later."

Destiny flung the invitation at his back and shrieked. "Let's talk about it *now*, Todd! I've given up everything to be with you and *I need to know now!*"

He turned and glared at her, his eyes shards of obsidian glass. "No one asked you to give up everything. You made a choice, now be a big girl and live with it!"

"You...selfish son of—"

"Watch your mouth," he warned, flinging a chinchilla wrap at her. "Put this on. It may get chilly later."

"I'm not going," she said defiantly, knowing just how much it would irritate him.

Todd wanted to slap her. He didn't know what was going on with her lately, but he was getting fed up fast. Even their physical relationship had grown stale. The only thing she *was* good for these days was publicity. But *love* her? What was that all about? What more did she want from him? They were living together, which was as close to love or marriage as he was trying to get for the moment.

He'd had enough for one night. Shrugging his shoulders, he said, "Have it your way...and just for the record, nothing happened that night in Malibu. You were so drunk it would've been a waste of my time!" He had the satisfaction of seeing her eyes widen with shock before he slammed the door behind him. There would be plenty of starlets at the premiere and any one of them would do. Destiny could stay home and cool off. Her absence would probably cause some speculation amongst the media since it was such an important premiere, but he didn't care. The publicity was what he'd been after and he already had what he wanted.

Chapter 45

"We're going house hunting and wanted to know if you'd like to join us," Mike said, waving at Ulla in her booster seat. The house they'd been temporarily renting had been sold and they had a month to vacate.

"I don't know, I've got a lot of stuff to do," Terri hedged. It was a couple of months after the anniversary party, but her pride was still smarting and she wasn't quite ready to forgive him yet.

"Oh, come on! It's Saturday, the weather's beautiful and I've got your biggest fan waiting inside the Tahoe."

"It is nice out. Where'd you plan on looking?"

"You know me. I'm sort of partial to waterfront property and there's this refurbished cape in Freeport that I've had my eye on."

"What happened with the house you were renting?" she asked.

"It was sold by the owner. We've got four weeks to vacate, which I think is more than fair. Anyway, it's time to purchase a home of my own. By the way, somebody misses you terribly." Ulla was in the first grade at a private school and Mike's job had allowed him to adjust his schedule so that he could be home from work by the time the school bus dropped her off.

Terri folded her arms and glanced guiltily at the SUV. She had decided to quit working for Mike shortly after the anniversary party.

Mike looked directly in her eyes. "I miss you, too. Look, I'm not asking you to move back in—"

"Good, because that's not going to happen."

"Will you let me finish?"

"Go ahead," she said.

"I'm just asking you to come spend the day with us and look at a couple of places. I think it would be fun for the three of us to do it together."

"I have to think about it. I'm supposed to visit my sister, Natalia, in East Elmhurst for a few days."

"You're running out of excuses," Mike felt obliged to point out.

"She just had triplets."

"Good one," he grudgingly admitted, "but I'm still not letting you off the hook that easily. By the way, how many sisters do you have?"

"Four and they all live in different parts of Queens."

"No further questions," he said with an amused gleam in his eyes. "So, are you coming, or what?"

"Does this little expedition of yours include lunch?"

"Absolutely."

"Okay, then I'm in! But, I can't go like this," she complained, pushing back the stray tendrils that had escaped her ponytail and glancing down at her track suit.

"You look great just the way you are," he said with a warm smile. "You might want to lose the pencil stuck behind your ear, though."

Terri smiled back faintly, hoping in her heart that she wasn't setting herself up for more disappointment.

Chapter 46

"Well, now the party can get started 'cause the entertainment has finally arrived!" exclaimed a stunning, gently tanned brunette in a white Valentino mermaid gown and a fortune in Van Cleef & Arpels diamonds.

Startled, Destiny swung her head around at the familiar voice. "Savannah Moore!" she squealed with delight.

The two old friends rushed to embrace one another, ignoring the curious stares of fellow party-goers. Savannah was one of the hottest commodities in Hollywood and one of the first people to really befriend Destiny when she first came to town. It was rumored that Savannah's husband, a world renowned film producer, had paved the way for her, but Savannah could care less about the gossip mills. The *Golden Globes*, *Oscars* and *People's Choice Awards* she had won on her own merit and she was a firm believer in not allowing good connections to go to waste. In fact, Savannah had been the one to put in a good word for Destiny's first big movie role, although she would never let her friend know it.

"Can I borrow her?" Savannah asked, plucking Destiny away from a hovering Todd. "I promise I'll bring her back."

Todd smiled coolly and kissed Savannah on either cheek. "You girls have fun."

Savannah grabbed Destiny by the hand and hustled her up a flight of marble stairs into an unoccupied guest room.

Destiny laughed. "You obviously know your way around the place."

"Belonged to a former beau," Savannah said by way of explanation, as she shut the door behind them. "Believe me, I'm well acquainted with quite a number of the rooms in this house!"

"You look great!" Destiny exclaimed, sitting down on the edge of an animal print chaise.

"So do you, as always. *I* had some work done," Savannah confided, blinking her wrinkle-free, green eyes and patting her décolletage. "Enough about me, though! Whatever are you doing with that cad?"

Destiny looked like the wind had been knocked out of her. Savannah Moore was notorious for not mincing words.

"Oh, honey, I didn't mean to upset you! It's just that you've been down *that* road before and you deserve better. God, if I had your youth and your looks—well, let's just say that I'd be giving that self-centered so-and-so his walking papers *and* the tabloids something to talk about! I was shocked to hear that the two of you were an item again! What happened to that delectable man of the law on the East Coast who swept you off your feet?"

"Todd happened," Destiny sullenly replied.

"Well, I have to tell you...you two look miserable together."

"Thanks, Savannah."

"I'm sorry, honey, but it's true! There's something strained and uncomfortable about the two of you. I didn't know whether to hug you or give you an enema! Don't get me wrong, you're still a stunning couple to *look* at...you just look like you'd rather be somewhere else...especially you."

"I would," Destiny said wistfully.

"So, what's the problem?" Savannah asked. "Life's too short, darling. If you like the East Coast better, then you need to hop a plane! Want to borrow my jet?"

"No, thanks. I don't think he's interested, Savannah," Destiny said with a catch in her voice, her eyes shimmering with unshed tears.

"Honey, how will you ever know for sure if you don't look him up and ask him? Seems to me that you've wasted enough time! I think you've got some soul searching to do. Now, let's go back downstairs before Mr. Hamilton sends security looking for us!"

Chapter 47

Two weeks later, Destiny accompanied Todd to his favorite French restaurant. She hoped that a romantic night out would help salvage whatever was left of their deteriorating relationship, but Todd wasn't making it easy. "Wasn't that the leading lady from the movie that got you an Oscar nod a few years ago?" Destiny asked, looking over her shoulder with a bewildered expression.

Todd hardly spared the Latin beauty a glance, but Destiny was certain the actress had noticed them coming into the restaurant and she looked a bit embarrassed by her former co-star's lack of acknowledgement. He took Destiny's hand and made a beeline for their usual reserved table on the other side of the upscale restaurant.

After sitting down in a chair which their waiter had pulled out for her, Destiny pinned Todd with a look. "Okay, what was all that about?"

"Nothing for you to concern yourself with," he coolly responded, perusing the wine list.

"Arc you having an affair with her?" Destiny prodded, her sharp eyes watching him for telltale signs.

"I *had* an affair with her," he said straight faced. "It was while I was dating that Greek model a few years ago. Read: before you and I got back together—so you can stop hurling daggers at me with your eyes."

"If that's the case, then why does she look so upset?"

"Because she didn't want it to end."

"Why did it end?"

"She got pregnant and wanted to get married," he replied, signaling their waiter who was standing at a very discreet distance. "As if that's a good enough reason to acquire a ball and chain," he said under his breath.

"You have a kid?" Destiny gasped.

"Will you please keep your voice down!" he hissed and then ordered a bottle for them in flawless French.

Destiny held her peace until the waiter was out of earshot

and then glared at Todd. "After all the flack you've given me about my kid—you hypocrite!"

"Get a grip, Destiny. I told her it was over and advised her to have an abortion. Whether or not she did it is a moot point."

"*A moot point?*" she asked incredulously. "How can you say that about your own flesh and blood?"

"Like I said, I advised her to have an abortion, so why don't you calm down and look at your menu before you completely ruin this evening?"

"I've suddenly lost my appetite," was her heated reply.

"Then, you can sit there and look cute, or pissed and watch me eat. *My* appetite's fine," he said, as he flipped open his menu.

"Apparently," she said. "I hope you choke," she murmured, leaning close so that she was in his face.

"Destiny," he said in a warning tone. "You're making a big deal out of nothing. Do not make a scene."

"I don't plan to. But right now, I'd rather eat at a fast food joint than sit here with you!" she exclaimed, rising from her seat.

Todd was tempted to grab her by the wrist and slam her back down into her chair. He no longer knew how to handle her emotional outbursts lately without things getting physical, so he watched her get up and storm toward the front of the restaurant, where the head waiter nearly tripped over himself to hold the door open for her. Then, Todd sucked in his breath, as Destiny abruptly changed direction and walked over to the section of the restaurant where his former co-star was dining with her companions...

The Latin actress glanced up with surprise, as Destiny approached her table.

Destiny politely extended her hand for the other woman to shake. "I apologize for interrupting your meal. We haven't been formally introduced, but my name is—"

"Destiny," the actress said with a hesitant smile. "I am a huge fan."

"And you are Iris Rodriguez. I'm a fan of yours, as well."

"Would you care to join us?"

"Thank you for your hospitality, but I'm actually on my way home. I just wanted to know if I could speak with you privately for a moment."

"Of course. Ladies, please excuse us," Iris said to her dinner companions, who were watching the exchange with wide eyes. "Where shall we go?"

"Some place with a bit of privacy, if that's okay with you."

"No problem," Iris said graciously.

They walked in silence to the restaurant's semi-deserted anteroom and Destiny stopped beside a softly illuminated settee and turned to face the Latin beauty.

"Iris, I want to apologize for Todd's behavior a short while ago. Regardless of whatever occurred between the two of you, that was uncalled for."

"Thank you, but unfortunately, I'm already used to Todd's behavior. One minute he's hot for you and the next—" the young woman suddenly blushed furiously when she recalled that she was speaking to Todd's current partner.

"Don't stress yourself, Iris. My relationship with Todd is…well…let's just say that our days are numbered. I just wanted to tell you that I made the mistake of abandoning my baby once for him and no man is worth it. Somehow I can't picture you choosing a man over your child—"

"Children," Iris said faintly, her eyes misting over.

"Children?" Destiny echoed with unbelief.

"Twins. A boy and a girl. They're being raised in another country by my family, far away from the spotlight and this crazy lifestyle I've chosen. That's why I frequently leave America for months. It's not to make more films."

Destiny slowly exhaled. "He doesn't know, does he?"

"No," Iris said frankly. "Todd made it very clear that he was not interested in being a father. I allowed him to think that I had an abortion, but I went back to my country, stayed during the second and third trimesters and delivered the babies there, as well."

"Don't you miss them?"

"All the time. Do you want to see pictures?" Iris asked, digging inside her purse for a miniature brag book. She located it and handed it to Destiny.

Destiny gasped as she flipped through it. Todd's babies should have been doing print ads. "Iris, they're beautiful *and* identical! Who is who?" Destiny asked, admiring one particular picture of the children as infants.

"The one on the left is Antonio and the one on the right is Angela—but we call her 'Angelita'," Iris said beaming with maternal pride.

"You should tell him," Destiny said firmly.

"Not a good idea. Todd is not a family man."

Destiny looked down at the photos of the cherubic twins and made up her mind.

She was about to make a scene. A big one.

"Alright—if you won't, then I will!"

"Destiny…please…don't!" Iris exclaimed with a startled expression.

It was too late, Destiny was already striding purposefully back over to the dining area where Todd was seated with Iris on her heels. By now the majority of the patrons and the staff were watching expectantly and some actually whipped out their cell phones to record the drama or take pictures.

Destiny stormed up to Todd's table and slammed the babies' photos down on the ivory linen in front of him. "Here's your 'moot point,' you selfish jerk!" she said, as Iris stood dazed and trembling a few feet away. "Enjoy the rest of your meal!"

***

"I suppose you thought that little stunt you pulled at the restaurant was funny," Todd said with barely contained fury.

"The other diners seemed amused—I don't really care what you thought," Destiny said, as she flung the rest of her belongings into a designer suitcase.

"So where are you headed? Back to the East Coast and oblivion?" he sneered, his arms crossing an Armani-clad chest.

"What do you care?" she asked without missing a beat. "Seems to me that you've got bigger fish to fry…*daddy*." Todd rushed over and got directly in her face and for half a minute Destiny wondered if he dared to hit her. She knew that he wanted to and she almost wished that he would. "Do it. I dare you. I'll

176

have battered women from here to Brazil boycotting your films and oh, the fun I'll have slandering your name on the talk show circuit after I take out an order of protection—"

Todd gritted his teeth and lowered his hand, "You know what? You're doing *me* a favor—good riddance! But don't think for a second that the 'vette or the Neil Lane ring are following you out that door."

Destiny just stared at him. "How is it that I couldn't get past your looks long enough to see what a petty, selfish idiot you really are?"

"Because the content of my character was never the last thing on your mind when I had you on your back—" was his vulgar reply. "Six months from now no one will even remember your name."

"I'll take my chances," she shrugged, turning away from him to zip up the suitcase.

"The cop's moved on by now…probably to your nanny," Todd added as a parting shot.

"If that's true I wish them well," she replied with an ironic smile, as she shut her suitcase and walked out the door.

Chapter 48

It was going to be one of the must-see interviews of the year. Destiny was finally going to do an exclusive with a journalist that she respected. She was nervous, but felt strongly that it was something she needed to do for herself, her fans, and most of all for Ulla and Mike.

The day of the interview she did her best to relax, but baring her soul was unfamiliar territory which left her feeling uncomfortable and vulnerable. Everything from the makeup person to the lighting crew seemed to agitate her and twice she found herself on the verge of tears. Finally, with head held as high as she could manage, she smiled graciously at the journalist and waited for the first question. Everything was going well until they touched on her past.

"Destiny, your fans are divided on this one and I suppose the question on everyone's mind is *what in the world happened*? You were involved with Todd years ago and that relationship didn't have a happy ending. So, why would you abandon your husband, a man you once called your 'guardian angel' and your child to be with Todd again?"

"I'd like to say that I'm just human and people make mistakes, but that would be the easy way out. The fact is: I blew it. I had a wonderful man who loved and trusted me and I betrayed him."

"Is there anything you'd like to say to your fans watching at home?"

"Yes, I'd like to apologize to the fans who are angry, hurt and disappointed by my actions. I'm grateful for the years of love and support you've shown me and if I could turn back the clock I would definitely make some different choices."

The journalist gently touched Destiny's hand. "Is there something you'd like to say to Mike, if he's watching?"

Destiny thought that she'd be able to handle the interview, but it was turning out to be much more painful than she had anticipated. She tried to hold the wave of emotion back, but the more she envisioned Mike's face the harder it became. "I'm sorry," she said huskily, as her eyes suddenly welled up.

"It's okay," the journalist said with compassion after handing her a box of tissue. "Just imagine it's only the two of you here right now. What would you say to him?"

"Sorry doesn't always make everything alright," Destiny sniffled, her eyes and nose turning pink as she stared into the camera lens. "But I don't know what else to say. I wish I could wipe the slate clean…that I could've been the kind of wife and mother you and Ulla deserve. Please forgive me for failing you and for being a coward. For not believing that I could do it, for not fighting to have it all, because I really thought I couldn't. I thought that marriage and family were liabilities—I didn't realize what a precious gift the two of you were until it was too late. You are the love of my life and always will be."

The studio was absolutely silent as Destiny abruptly stood up and walked off the set. The journalist gave the signal to break for a commercial.

Stunned, Mike sat down slowly on his new sofa. He'd heard about the upcoming interview and had been determined not to watch it. Unfortunately, as he began to channel surf, he'd stumbled across it. He barely recognized the lovely, forlorn creature being interviewed. Five years after the fact, she still looked the same, but the devastation he saw in her eyes tugged at his heart strings. He changed the channel with an unsteady hand. After the interview aired, Ramirez, Mike's mother, and his sister called to speak with him about it and he let them all leave messages on his answering machine. He just couldn't go there tonight. Maybe not ever again.

Chapter 49

Destiny sat down on the bed in shock, as she stared at the front page of the paper. There was Todd with that starlet, who had recently been nominated for an Emmy, waving at the paparazzi from his father's yacht. The starlet was sporting a Neil Lane wedding band and a Dior gown that brides around the country would be clamoring for by week's end. There was also an awful inset photo of Destiny with the caption: *Out with the old, In with the new!*

She'd never seen it coming.

That jerk had actually *married* someone!

According to the article, Todd had met his bride at a recent movie premiere and it had been love at first sight. Yeah, right. The girl wasn't even his type! She was lanky, well-educated and despised the limelight. Todd liked his women curvy, fame hungry and camera friendly. It had to be a career-related move on his part, or maybe her family was simply 'old Hollywood' and he wanted the prestige. Destiny knew that it wasn't love, because the only person that Todd Hamilton loved was himself.

She actually felt sorry for his new wife: the girl was in for a rude awakening. Destiny gave their marriage six months and that was only because she was feeling generous.

***

The doorbell rang. The new personal assistant had the day off and the housekeeper was busy vacuuming. Destiny checked the surveillance camera and squealed. Racing to the front door, she flung it open, her eyes filled with tears as she hugged her old friend. "Chelsea! It took you long enough!"

"So, how are you holding up?" the former assistant asked dutifully.

"As well as can be expected," Destiny sniffled.

"It's not the end of the world, you know."

"I know. But this is the perfect time for a little break."

"I wouldn't run, if I were you. I'd tell them all to kiss my butt and act like everything was fine even if it was killing me!"

"That's *pride* and if I recall correctly, you said that was a sin. I'm just tired, right now and I need a change of scenery. I'll be fine."

"I told you he was no good," Chelsea muttered.

"Yeah, but for awhile I was *no good*, too."

"That's true. You wouldn't happen to be considering a trip to the East Coast, would you?"

"Why?"

"I'm just curious."

"No, you're not. You're trying to be in my business again."

"What can I say? Old habits die hard…"

"I might make a pit stop there, depending on how things go," she trailed off with a slight shrug of her shoulders.

"You're going to go see him, aren't you?" Chelsea asked enthusiastically.

"I'm going to Fifth Avenue to shop myself into a coma. That's about it."

"But if you should happen to bump into one of *New York's Finest…*"

"Please, Chelsea! That man's not thinking about me on his worst day."

"You'd be surprised."

"You know something I don't?" Destiny said dryly.

"I know that he'll always love you and that you're the mother of his baby. Nothing will ever change that, especially not that horse's rear end, Todd Hamilton!"

They exchanged a meaningful look and Destiny inexplicably felt her heart lighten. She squeezed her former assistant's hand in silent thanks. "It's good to have you back."

"What? I'm not on the payroll."

"You know what I mean!"

"Yeah, I know what you mean," Chelsea teased. "It's good to be back."

"So, who are you working for these days? Hopefully not another stuck-on-herself diva with a messed up personal life!"

"Not at the moment, but I'm keeping my eyes open!"

Chapter 50

"Hey, gorgeous. How are you?" Todd asked from behind a startled Destiny.

She just stared at him for a moment, wanting with all her heart to punch him in his arrogant face and break his Versace frames. She couldn't believe he had the nerve to come within twenty feet of her. Aware that more than one pair of curious eyes were upon them backstage at this latest awards show, she mentally counted to ten.

"I'm just peachy, Todd—and by the way, congrats," she added, smiling so broadly she was certain her jaw would crack.

"Thanks," he said, with that smirk she'd come to despise. "It was a spur of the moment thing."

"I'm sure it was," she nearly snorted. *He'd had 200 guests at his reception. How impromptu could it have been?*

"So, who are you presenting with tonight?" he asked, his mouth watering over the luminous Michael Kors gown she was wearing. His wife didn't look this good even after a team of stylists had finished with her. But, then, he hadn't married her for her looks.

"Vin Diesel," Destiny replied cheerily. He was one of her favorite actors and Todd knew it. "And you?"

"Some kid from the Disney channel who had a hit record and was suddenly an overnight sensation. I don't even remember her name."

Destiny almost snickered. Todd hated pop stars. Someone behind the scenes at that show had a great sense of humor.

"So, it's going to be a night to remember, after all," she said, cheesing it up for a photographer.

"It could be," he said with a suggestive look.

Was he out of his mind? "Wow, Todd. You're not even married four months yet. Hmmm, let me think," she said touching her chin. "You know what, I think I'll pass. Enjoy the rest of your life and tell the little woman she has my deepest sympathy."

"Is this guy bothering you?" Vin Diesel asked coming up

behind Todd.

"Vin!" she squealed, nearly knocking Todd over to give the actor a warm hug. "I thought you were going to stand me up."

"Not in a million years, doll and you didn't answer my question."

"Oh, him?" she asked appraising Todd coolly. "He was just leaving."

"Good," Diesel said, as he placed a protective arm around her waist. "Because three's a crowd."

Chapter 51

"Chelsea, look at this!" Destiny yelled, as she stared at the high-definition flat screen.

"What?"

"Will you come here—there's news on ET about Todd."

Chelsea snorted rudely from another room. "Oh, yeah, like hearing his name's going to make me get over there faster!"

"He got a divorce!" Destiny threw in.

Magically her rehired personal assistant appeared by her side. "Now, that's a horse of a different color! It's only been five months! What happened?"

"He got back together with Iris—"

"Ahh, the Brazilian Bombshell."

"And *they're* engaged."

"That should make his previous wife real happy," Chelsea said shaking her head. "I hope she drags his behind to the bank."

"I doubt that'll happen. I'm willing to bet that there were pre-nups drawn up before that trip down the aisle—especially on her side of the fence. I hear her family is loaded."

"I'll tell you one thing: that man sure does have a thing for our Latin sisters."

"Yeah—I still don't get why he was interested in me."

Chelsea just stared at Destiny. "If you haven't figured it out by now…"

The camera cut to a scene of Todd and Iris shopping on Rodeo Drive and zoomed in on the major bling on the actress's all-important digit.

"And I gave his first marriage six months," Destiny muttered.

"Technically, this is your fault," Chelsea replied.

"How?"

"That scene you made in the restaurant. The man had no idea that he had procreated until you slapped those babies' pictures down in front of his plate!"

"Somebody had to do it. Iris was too scared."

"You sure you weren't looking for an easy way out?"

Destiny rolled her eyes. "Maybe I was. But that relationship was already rolling downhill by the time that event took place."

"Well, I—for one—am glad that it finished rolling. By the way, that fine Greek director called, he wants to know if he can escort you to Diddy's birthday bash."

"Hmmm," Destiny said, pretending to give it some serious consideration.

"I wouldn't do it if I were you," Chelsea offered her two cents.

"But you're *not* me."

"The press would be all over the two of you like—"

"Chelsea, don't you ever give it a rest?" Destiny asked incredulously. The old Destiny would have accepted that invitation in a heartbeat; the new Destiny was only interested in getting back to one man on the East Coast. "Please call him back, thank him and let him know that I'm going out of town for awhile, so I won't be able to accept his invitation."

"Good answer," Chelsea said with an approving nod. "When should I book the flight to New York?"

"Today, please. I think I'd like to be there by Friday."

"Will you be staying at the condo?" Chelsea asked.

"That depends…"

"LGA or JFK?"

"MacArthur."

"Not wasting any time, are you?"

"I've already done plenty of that. Wouldn't you agree?"

Chelsea grinned. *No one could tell her that prayer didn't work!*

"I'm going to pack."

"Sounds like a plan. I'll be making reservations if you need me."

Destiny reached for the platinum, diamond and aquamarine ring nestled in the soft velvet of her jewelry box and slid it on her ring finger; it felt so comfortable there. She admired the fiery sparkle of it from different angles for a few minutes and then placed it inside a protective travel pouch.

So you'll always remember me.

That's what Mike had said the day he slipped it on her finger.

When Todd found out that she still had her engagement ring and wedding band he had gone out and purchased a sapphire designer confection that almost blinded her. Non-engagement, of course. It had been stunning, but lacked the warmth and sentiment of Mike's ring.

Mike had refused to take his rings back when they divorced. Todd made sure that he got his ring back the same day they split.

Actions definitely spoke louder than words.

Too bad that sometimes she had been hard of hearing.

But, that was all about to change. If Mike was home and if he would even allow her through the front door.

Chapter 52

"Destiny," Mike said, feeling a familiar tightening in his chest; she was more beautiful at that moment than he could remember. Why did she keep popping in and out of his life like this? And when was he going to stop letting her in every time she did it?

"I was in town. May I come in?"

He slowly stepped aside and then scanned the area outside his house for scoop-hungry press. "No entourage?"

"Not this weekend," she said with a little smile that did weird things to his insides. Even with her hair in a ponytail, low-waist jeans and Nine West ankle boots she looked fantastic. Nobody filled out a pair of jeans the way Destiny did.

"Would you like something to drink?"

"Thanks. Some tea would be nice. Do you have herbal?"

"Sure, that's all we used to—" he trailed off awkwardly. "What are you doing here?"

"I needed to speak with you in person," she said, suddenly fearful that he would throw her out.

"After all this time?"

"Where is everybody?" she asked, evading his question.

"Ulla's spending the weekend with my family and Terri's out of town."

"So we're alone..."

Mike didn't answer her, but turned and began walking away. "The kitchen's down the hall to your right. Why don't you put some water on? I'm going to finish taking my shower."

Destiny stood indecisively in the middle of the floor. Part of her wanted to follow Mike; part of her didn't know how he would respond if she did. She was just grateful he hadn't slammed the front door in her face. For now the tea kettle was looking like the wisest way to go.

"You look terrific," Destiny mentioned after a sip of Wild Berry Zinger. Mike was wearing a navy NYPD logo tee and matching sweatpants. "Still working out, I see."

"Four days a week minimum. But that's not what you came here to tell me, so spill," he said, as he rubbed his damp hair with a fluffy monogrammed towel. One of their wedding gifts he didn't have the heart to part with.

"I just wanted to talk…"

"You came all the way out to Long Island to *talk*? You could've phoned, you know."

"I know." Was he going to make her spell everything out for him?

Mike sat down on the sofa across from her, pinning her with that breathtaking aquamarine gaze. "What's going on, Destiny?"

"Everything…nothing," she sputtered, then jumped up from her chair and walked over to a bay window in the living room. "This is a terrific house. How close are you to the beach?"

"Less than 10 minutes."

"Can we go?"

"Destiny…"

"Please, Mike. It's really important."

He stared at his ex-wife quizzically and then went to get the keys to his Tahoe.

Mike didn't know how long they sat on the dunes staring out at the ocean, but at some point the temperature began to drop, so he went back to the SUV to grab a nautical-themed throw to place around Destiny's shoulders. It was only mid-September, but the days already seemed shorter and cooler. The beach itself was deserted except for an occasional jogger or resident out walking their dog.

"Remember the first time you brought me here?" she asked softly, as if speaking normally would ruin the moment.

"How could I forget? You were terrified that the sand would ruin your Jimmy Choos!" Mike reflected, glancing into her beautiful eyes as the setting sun flecked the perimeters with gold.

"That was the first time you kissed me."

"If I recall correctly, the night you invited me backstage to that video shoot was the first time I kissed you."

"Oh, right! I was something, wasn't I?"

"Yeah, but I didn't really mind," he admitted.

"Would you mind now?" she asked hesitantly.

Mike gazed longingly at her full lips and then looked away.

Destiny's eyes filled with tears. "I'm so sorry, Mike. Please forgive me."

"I've already forgiven you—you need to forgive yourself."

"How can I? For that matter, how can you?"

"It's simple—I hated the things you'd done, but I never once stopped loving you."

"You're a better person than I am."

"No," he sighed, "I'm not. Jesus loves unconditionally and that's the way I'm striving to love. He forgives me when I mess up, so who am I to hold a grudge forever?"

"You have every right to. You didn't deserve anything I put you through."

"Yeah, well, Jesus didn't deserve to go to the cross, either..."

"Still religious, huh?" she asked tilting her head.

"Religious, no. A believer, definitely. I know that it's only my faith in God that got me through the past few years."

"And it was your faith that drew me to you," she acknowledged for the first time.

"So it wasn't my good looks?" he teased, warmed for some odd reason by her comment.

"Your looks definitely didn't repel me, but there was something about you...your morals, values, and beliefs. I found you irresistible. I would have done just about anything to be with you."

"Are you hungry?" Mike asked abruptly, changing the subject. He remembered that look on her face and knew where the conversation could lead.

"The truth or a lie?" she asked mischievously.

"Come on," he said, brushing sand from his sweatpants and extending his hand to her.

190

"Where are we headed, Officer Reilly?"

"Nautical Mile. You look like you could use a bowl of fresh chowder."

Since it was the end of the tourist season, the restaurants on the Mile were relatively quiet. Mike chose one of his favorite spots and requested a secluded table far from the doors and windows. He wasn't taking any chances with a surprise visit from the local media. When the hostess' eyes widened in recognition, he immediately gave her a look which let her know that autograph requests would not be welcomed that evening. Fortunately, they were served by an older waitress whose only concern was what they wanted from the menu.

Afterwards, Mike and Destiny strolled to the end of the Mile where a wooden gazebo overlooked the choppy, moonlit water. Jazz from an outside eatery swayed invitingly on the briny breeze. It was one of those nights when the very air was teeming with possibilities.

Partially concealed by the gazebo's shadows, Mike turned hesitantly toward Destiny, his fingers aching to move the honey-colored tendrils that were blowing gently across her face...the darkness concealing his indecision.

Destiny closed her eyes and prayed. She needed this man to kiss her like she needed her next breath. When she felt him take a step back she had to force herself to not stomp her foot in protest.

"Maybe we should call it a night," he finally murmured.

"Why?" she asked, tremulously.

"Because you're *you* and I don't trust *me*."

"I promise to respect you in the morning," she lightly vowed.

"You're something else. How did we ever end up together?"

"I needed rescuing and you were my knight in shining armor."

"Oh, yeah," he replied, with a smile that didn't quite reach his eyes. "Come on, it's time to go."

"Why didn't you kiss me?" Destiny blurted once they

were back inside the Tahoe.

"I didn't want to risk things getting out of hand."

"Would it be so awful if things had gotten out of hand?"

"We're divorced, Destiny. Lusting after you caused me a lot of heartache in the past…that's not a road I want to go down again. Did you want to kiss me because your boyfriend's out of the picture?"

Destiny pretended she wasn't caught off guard by that question. "You should catch up on your tabloid reading. He's been *out of the picture* for awhile."

"What happened?"

"He was just using me," she frankly replied. "And when he was finished he decided it was time to move on to someone else who would keep him in the media's spotlight."

Mike was silent. The thought of anyone using the mother of his child and kicking her to the curb like yesterday's trash upset him. Still, Destiny had reaped what she had sown.

"So it took his hooking up with someone else for you to realize what an idiot he was?"

"I'd convinced myself that he had changed," she shrugged. "Besides, I knew it was already too late for us."

"Where are you staying?"

"Nowhere at the moment. I flew in to MacArthur and drove a rental right over to your place."

"What happened to the condo?"

"I still own it. I just haven't been there in a long time."

"Well, it's safer than staying at a hotel. We'll swing by my house and pick up the rental and then I'll drive you into the city." Mike put the key in the ignition, his expression neutral. Inwardly he was still cringing at the thought of her flying commercial— even if it was first class—and driving around without proper security. *Would she never learn?*

Destiny laid her hand on his. "If it's alright with you, I'm not in a hurry to leave. Would it be okay if we just hung out a while longer and talked?"

He turned the ignition off and relaxed in his seat. "What would you like to talk about?"

192

"Us," she said with a catch in her voice.

"I thought we both said plenty today," he replied carefully.

She unbuckled her seatbelt and turned to face him. "I thought we'd just gotten started."

"We were civil and are obviously still attracted to one another. It doesn't mean anything, Destiny."

"You know something, Officer Reilly? You were never a liar."

He stopped staring out at the wharf long enough to frown at her. "What's that supposed to mean?"

"That it's time to start being truthful. I love you and I miss you. I made a terrible mistake and it cost us, but I'm willing to do whatever it takes to make it up to you and Ulla."

"We can never have what we once had. I don't trust you anymore, Destiny."

"No, but you still love me," she said softly, ignoring the heartache his honesty had caused. "I can see it in your eyes and feel it when you're holding me."

"What do you want me to say?" he asked, gesturing with his hands.

"I want you to listen to your heart for five minutes—I'm finally listening to mine!" she whispered fiercely, with glistening eyes.

Mike looked away. He had never been more afraid in his entire life. This woman had the power to wound him like no one else could, yet he loved her with every fiber of his being. He had fooled himself into believing that she was out of his system, because all he wanted to do at that moment was hold her and kiss her until they were both out of breath. He was at a loss when she started to cry. To invite Destiny back into his life could be spiritual and emotional suicide.

Love covers a multitude of sins…

The scripture came to him from out of the blue.

Yeah, but how much sin was it supposed to cover? He wondered bluntly.

Temporarily placing his thoughts on a mental backburner, Mike laced his fingers through hers and squeezed gently. "It's going to be okay, Destiny."

"No it's not," she sputtered, resting her head upon his chest. "How could I have been so stupid?"

"Just let it go."

"I can't—I abandoned Ulla...hurt and humiliated you..."

"We'll get through this," he vowed.

"*We*? I don't deserve your help," she abruptly pulled away, leaving a big wet spot on his sweatshirt. "Why are you being so nice?"

Mike took her chin in his hand and looked in her eyes. "Because I love you. Always have, always will, no matter what. Now let's get out of here before this ends up online somewhere."

It had started raining by the time they returned to Mike's house. They dashed inside with the nautical throw covering their heads. Mike got a fire started and Destiny went to put the kettle on for tea and hot chocolate.

***

"We've eaten, watched a movie and played five rounds of *Jenga*. What would you like to do now?" Mike asked, ever the perfect host.

Destiny looked up at him from the mountain of cushy pillows on the living room floor and then extended her hand to him. "Just to be with you."

Mike took her hand and reclined on the pillows beside her, trying to push back the memories of their last encounter. "Your hair's almost dry," he said, inspecting one of the long dark gold strands.

"It dries pretty fast—"

"I remember," he replied, the firelight reflected in his aquamarine gaze.

"I should probably comb it out before it starts to tangle."

"That's not a bad idea. I'll get a comb."

"Wait!" she implored. "Don't leave. You know how much I hate it when you leave."

"This isn't a good idea, Destiny."

"What?"

"I suppose you've forgotten about the last time we were

together like this."

She looked away, chewing on her bottom lip. "I'm sorry about that. I shouldn't have run out on you that way."

"You shouldn't have run out on me at all!" he replied, before he could catch himself. "I thought you were going to be there the next day…that we would work things out…but you left without saying a word. I felt like an idiot, Destiny and I felt used. You came and got what you needed and left me hanging. I didn't appreciate that."

"I'm sorry…but now I'm here," she said with a small voice. "And I'll stay as long as you want me to." She wanted everything to work out so badly she was shaking.

How could she have let this man slip through her fingers?

"Mike," she whispered, her eyes mirroring her soul.

"Yeah?" he asked. Emotions were churning through him at a dizzying pace and he was aching to kiss and hold her again; his body was already responding to her nearness.

"Why didn't you just ignore my request and take me home?"

"Honestly? I was enjoying your company."

"I have another question. Something I meant to ask you a long time ago. What were you thinking the first day we met? Did you know who I was when I hopped inside your car?"

"Yes," he finally answered. "I knew who you were and I thought that you were prettier in person than on television."

"Just prettier?" she asked with a little frown.

"Look, I was just grateful that there was no traffic that day! I was more concerned about your safety than your looks."

"So when did you realize that you were attracted to me?" she prodded.

"What is this, an interrogation?" he joked.

"It's important," she said with an odd expression. "Please try to humor me."

"I was attracted to you from day one, especially in your condo, when you were putting the moves on me."

Destiny smiled at the memory.

"Eventually I realized that no matter how many times I

tried to take a stand and keep you at arms length—"

"—I was *your* Delilah," she murmured, recalling that fateful night Ulla was conceived and Destiny had caused her guardian angel to fall.

Mike nodded solemnly. He had always accepted his role in the sin, along with the consequences.

"That Dolce & Gabbana gown that I wore to the show that night didn't help," Destiny reflected.

"None of your gowns ever helped," he said frankly.

"Sorry about that," she said sincerely. "It's part of the star package: they design 'em and I promote 'em"

Not for the first time that evening they lapsed into an uneasy silence, both wanting to say more, but afraid to.

Thunder suddenly boomed outside, rattling the window panes and flashes of lightning illuminated the sky. The house lights flickered for a moment as though they were about to go out completely.

"Whoa. They didn't say anything about this in the forecast. How about I take you home tomorrow when it's safe to be out there?"

"Only if you promise to make me breakfast."

"Fully-loaded omelets just the way you like 'em," he promised.

"And bacon?"

"Not too crunchy, scout's honor," he vowed.

"Where will I be sleeping tonight?"

"In the guest room," Mike said as he helped her up from the floor. He led her down a hallway to a cozy room outfitted with a quilted bedspread, shams, eyelet skirt and hurricane lamps. "Don't say a word. This was my mother's idea."

"What? I like it," she said with a little shrug.

"There are toiletries in the adjoining bathroom," Mike informed her. "I'll see you in the morning."

"Hey," she said lightly touching his forearm.

"Yeah?" Mike asked turning to look back at her and trying to ignore how seriously appealing she was sans makeup and the diva wardrobe.

196

"Thanks for everything. You didn't have to let me in." She leaned forward to kiss him on the cheek and Mike stepped backward involuntarily.

"You're welcome. Now get some rest." He quickly shut the door behind him and exhaled.

Chapter 53

Terri couldn't wait to see Mike. She must have been doing 85 on the Long Island Expressway. She had to tell him the truth. Their "friendly" relationship was bogus and it wasn't working for her. She was deeply in love with him and had to know the truth about how he felt and she had to know today. Mike needed her in his life and Ulla needed a mother. Besides, Terri's older sister's kids were driving her up the wall. It was either move out, or go nuts.

There was no time to pull into the driveway, she parked her orange Cobalt in front of the newly refurbished cape and fished around in her purse for Mike's emergency house keys...

"Hey, Bill. No, I'm not in Manhattan yet, I'm still on the Island...believe it or not ...none of your business, nosey! Kelly still wants me on the show? Cool. I know that you've already rescheduled me, you're the best...I'll be there...call you afterwards, okay? Smooches, to you, too. Bye."

"What are *you* doing here?"

Destiny spun around at the strained, but familiar voice. She felt like kicking herself for not getting dressed right after her shower. Confronting an irate rival in her ex-husband's NYPD logo tee was not her idea of fun. "Hello to you, too, Terri."

"I asked you a question!" Terri exploded, dropping her luggage on the hardwood floor.

"I don't owe you any explanations. This is still *my* family and you're still the hired help!"

"I don't work for you any more!"

"Don't forget that I'm the one who hired you. You might want to watch your tone and show some respect."

"*Respect?!* Were you respecting them when you were lying topless on some beach in St. Tropez with your co-star, or when you were caught with him in some fitting room on Rodeo Drive? Were you respecting them while you were club hopping in LA? *Don't you ever talk to me about respect!* You don't respect yourself and you certainly don't respect this family! I've been

Ulla's mother! I was the one who got up at three o'clock in the morning to warm those bottles! I was the one who took her to the pediatrician and who paced the floor with her when she was teething! I was the one at the *Mommy & Me* classes! Where in the hell have you been for the past six years?!"

Mike hurried down the hallway to find out what was going on. He stopped in his tracks when he saw Terri. She wasn't due back in town for three more days and he could've sworn that he'd told her to only use the spare keys in case of emergency.

She glared at him through her tears. "I don't have to ask whether or not you had a good weekend!" she exclaimed, giving Destiny a scathing look. "I hope she was worth it!"

"Terri, wait," he said, adjusting the belt on his bathrobe. He entreated Destiny with a look and she left them alone and went back down the hallway to the guestroom.

"For what, Mike? To pick up the pieces once she breaks your heart again? Haven't you learned anything?!"

"She's still the mother of my child. She has a right to be here."

"No, Mike. She's a disgrace of a woman and a poor excuse for a parent, but you'll *never* see that!"

"Stop, don't leave like this," he implored.

"I have to, Mike. You'll never care for anyone the way you care for her! I'm tired of living in Destiny's shadow!"

"You're not living in her shadow."

Terri snorted rudely. "Why couldn't you just be honest and tell me that you still had feelings for her? Why did you have to lead me on?"

"I never led you on!"

"You kissed me and told me that you care about me—that's not leading me on?"

Mike slammed the door shut, as she opened it. "I do care, Terri. That wasn't a lie. I didn't plan for this to happen."

"Did it ever occur to you that maybe she did?" Terri huffed, her eyes blurry with tears.

"She just came by to talk."

"Six years after the fact? Why didn't she just have her

pricey lawyers do it?"

"Do you want me to say I'm sorry? Is that what this is all about?"

"No, because *sorry* just won't cut it. Tell me something," she sobbed, turning to face him. "Did you sleep with her?"

"No."

"But you wanted to, didn't you?"

"Yes," he admitted. "And I won't apologize for that. We were married and we have a child."

"Gee, Mike, thanks for reminding me…"

He closed his eyes and sighed heavily, as she slammed the front door behind her.

A short while later, Destiny placed a gentle hand on his shoulder. "I'm going to go. You look like you've got a lot on your mind."

Mike ran his fingers through his hair and turned to face her. He hated what had just happened and needed to fix things. He wasn't in love with Terri, but he could have been.

Destiny read the indecision and struggle in his eyes. She wasn't going to miss the boat again. "Listen, before I go, there's something I want to say." She paused before plunging ahead, unaware that she was trembling. "You once told me to take a peek inside the Bible, that I'd be amazed. Well, I did and I was amazed at how many love stories are in it…but I was more amazed about how much forgiveness is in it. Whatever you decide, I won't rush you and I will respect your decision. Take care of yourself."

Speechless, Mike stared at the door after she left.

How in the world was he supposed to choose?

Chapter 54

One year later, Mike showed up at Destiny's building. He'd heard through the grapevine that the West Coast had lost its appeal and that Destiny was on hiatus for at least a year. She had fired her agent, hired Chelsea to manage her, and was only interested in Big Apple gigs since she wanted to spend more time with their daughter. He had to give her credit: she hadn't pursued him or tried to coerce him to make any decisions. She picked their child up on weekends and dutifully attended every PTA meeting, recital, and play date her busy schedule allowed. It was almost as though she was trying to make up for lost time...

He nodded cordially at the doormen, and went directly up to the security console. The guards looked surprised when they saw him. All except one. It was an older guard who had been praying from the very beginning that the song bird and the police officer would make it. He smiled at Mike and shook the younger man's hand. "Good to see you again, Officer Reilly."

"Thanks, Isaiah. If she's available, would you please let her know that I'm here?"

Destiny was startled when her house phone rang. It was building security. Mike was downstairs. She instructed them to send him right up.

She began pacing the floor of her condo, a mug of herbal tea cooling on the kitchen counter. Mike was here! He *never* came by her place anymore. She always picked Ulla up from his house and dropped her back off. He was so decent. He had probably just come to tell her in person that he and Terri had finally decided to make things official.

But what if they wanted to move away? What if they wanted to take Ulla with them? Could she handle letting her only child go, even if it was an opportunity for her to have a real family?

Destiny was already crying when she opened the door.

Mike immediately put a bouquet of calla lilies down on a

delicately carved table and sheltered her within his arms.

When the sobbing had subsided, she gazed gratefully up at him. "You didn't have to make a special trip. You could've called me. I know that you've made your decision…"

What she didn't know was that Mike had spent a year fasting, praying, and seeking the heart of God. He had to be sure that this time around he was being motivated by what was in his spirit and not his emotions or his flesh. God finally showed him Destiny in a dream, luminous, in a gown whiter than snow and said, *"Behold thy wife!"* That was all the confirmation he needed.

"Beloved," he whispered, stroking her hair. "You *are* my decision. I have loved you with an everlasting love and I'm not about to stop now." He gazed at her tenderly and then kissed her the way he did that very first time, so many years ago. Letting her know exactly how he had always felt about her. That she alone was his destiny, now and forever.

Epilogue

"Mike? Is that you?"

He turned around abruptly, almost spilling his latte. "Terri?" he said with disbelief. She looked fantastic. Gone was the tidy, but ordinary ponytail she'd frequently worn and the nondescript college student clothing. Her wardrobe had gotten a major overhaul and she even had makeup on. "Hey, you look fantastic!" He wasn't going to add that he almost didn't recognize her.

"Thanks," she said pleased with the compliment.

"And your hair—"

"It was time for an upgrade," she smiled, as she flicked straight, razor-layered tresses over one shoulder. "I'm headed over to Lexington, which way are you going?"

"Same direction. Mind if I tag along?"

"Of course not, the more the merrier! How's my former charge doing?"

"Getting taller, smarter and prettier every day. I'm a little biased since I think she's perfect."

"And Destiny?"

"Is born-again and regularly attending church."

Terri kept her expression neutral. There was no need to ask if they had remarried, it had taken weeks for the internet buzz to die down. What he kindly didn't mention was that Destiny was also five months pregnant with his son. "That's wonderful news!" she finally replied with a plastered-on smile.

"She recently did voiceover work in an animated movie and was asked to star in a new Broadway show."

"Wow, isn't God awesome?"

"All the time! Terri, if you don't mind my asking, what brings you to this neck of the woods?"

"My fiancé, Josh. We're going to the movies as soon as he finishes work. I'm sort of twisting his arm about seeing a romantic comedy, but he's pushing for something with car chases and a heavy conspiracy storyline."

"An action junkie, huh? Congrats! I'm happy for you." She flashed him the rock on her left hand and he whistled appreciatively.

"Thanks, it happened New Year's Eve."

"Where'd you meet him?"

"At school, believe it or not. Remember that date who told me to look him up when I became available again?"

"No kidding," Mike laughed. "The poor guy who listened to how much you loved your job all night on your first date."

"That's the one! We even go to the same church!"

"God has a sense of humor."

"Definitely. Hey, listen, I uh—please forgive me!" Terri blurted, pausing on a quiet street strewn with refurbished brownstones.

"For what?" Mike asked with a baffled expression.

"When I rededicated my life to Christ, God spoke with me about my role in everything that happened. Nobody told me to fall in love with you. I was your employee first, then your friend. I had no right to judge Destiny or lay a guilt trip on you for not getting over your wife. I should've been praying for your family, not trying to keep it for myself."

"Don't place the entire blame on yourself. I was so angry with God after everything went down and it wasn't like I was pushing you away."

"I guess we both had a lot of spiritual growing up to do," she concluded. They continued walking a few more avenues in companionable silence, each lost in their own thoughts until Terri finally paused in front of an office building that appeared as old as Manhattan itself. "Well, this is me."

"Looks like a landmark," Mike noted, admiring the architecture.

"I believe it is…it was great running into you, Mike."

"Same here," he said, squeezing her hand warmly, knowing that a hug might have been too awkward. "Congrats, again."

"You, too. Give Ulla a kiss for me, okay?"

"Will do. Take care of yourself."

"You, too…"

Inside the shiny, air-conditioned lobby, Terri waved at the security guard seated at the console and pressed the elevator button with a shaky hand. She reached for the key ring inside her blazer pocket and touched the plastic covered photo of Ulla, Mike and herself posing in front of the Bethesda Fountain. She knew that she should've gotten rid of the thing a long time ago…

Terri bit her bottom lip, startled by an unexpected wave of emotion. Mike had been her first love, a man she could envision spending the rest of her life with. But his heart had belonged to someone else. Terri knew that she would always have a special, secret place in her own heart for him, but he wasn't her present or her future.

As the elevator doors silently opened, she wiped her eyes and walked purposefully down the hallway toward her fiancé's office, choosing to believe by faith that everyone was exactly where they were supposed to be. She had her own destiny to fulfill and a God who was big enough to help her get there.

www.ingramcontent.com/pod-product-compliance
Lightning Source LLC
Chambersburg PA
CBHW071200260626
47162CB00003B/1124